Don't Blink

a collection of short stories

Z. J. Sciales

Copyright 2024 by Zachary John Sciales

A Bright Night Press publication.
The very first, if you're curious.

Cover and illustrations by the coveted and illustrious Nathan Ebersole.

Edited by the brilliant and jarringly insightful Eric Westerlind.

ISBN: 979-8-9920586-2-8

For Andrea,

the unfailing light in my life,

and

for my mother, father, and sister,

my original unflinching supporters.

Further Dedications

While I admit to no small amount of vanity in finally holding an ink and paper (flesh and blood?) version of something I've written, it only ever really exists for you. The eyes on the word, the word in the mind, the mind awhirl with possibility—leaping joy, tender fear, an unseemly snort of laughter, and the inevitable sprinkle of marinara across the page numbers.

All this to say, thank you for making it worthwhile. Thank you for considering this a worthwhile pursuit.

For a thousand reasons, the ghosts of unpublished works haunt all my hard drives and cloud drives. These stories felt different. They have a pulse humming along in their veins, some verve, something tingly and dark and engrossing.

They feel right. And so it feels right to "start" here, insofar as publishing is concerned, with these engaging shorter tales wrapped up in this elegant binding.

Nathan Ebersole illustrated both the vivid dustjacket art as well as the more subtle interior artwork. Many thanks for his patience and daring through that process.

And we all owe Eric Westerlind a debt of gratitude for reminding me that this is worth it. That there's more to good writing than the occasional poetic phrase and a well-timed poop joke. In short, thank you for editing these stories. Thank you for reminding me to fear and love the red pen.

Many of these tales went out rough, uncut, direct from the source, to a small audience who weighed, measured, and — this a shock to me, I assure you — continued to read. Even encouraged the endeavor. Asked for more. I cannot thank you all from a deep enough part of my heart for that belief and allowing me to plug up your inboxes with toilet emojis for a year.

That's why we're here, in print. Because you believed in it, and I found joy in it. We ran into one another on the page. A most thrilling collision.

And so, in that spirit of deepest gratitude for the fiction made flesh, let's raise a toast to the generous sponsors who breathed a little extra life into these pages. Here are your names, in the book:

Devin and Keri Cooney, Andrea Sciales, Andrew Gailey, Christa Yawney, Christian and Rachel Bennett, Chris and Emily Todd, Cory Schaefer, Cyrus Goudarzi, Daniel and Noah Abson, Diane and Doug Adams, Eric Westerlind, Evan Dupe, Eugene and Dr. Kathy DesLauriers, Hunter Harriss, Joyce Adams, Jennifer and Philip McSween, Karl Henricksen and Clarissa Duque, Kevin Kelly and Jia Jamal, Maddy Rushton, Madison and Kristen Traynham, Mary and David Stone, Matt, Matthew and Kelsey Krattenmaker, Meghan and Mike Garite, Michele and Chris Becker, Nathan Ebersole, Nick and Dr. Paige Sciales, Nick and Dr. Meaghan Ludlow, Dr. Nick and Daniela Masciello, Roland Ebersole, Sandie Huerkens, Stacy Ruml, Tessa, Dr. William Scott Bennett and Dede Bennett

Special thanks to the beloved Lunatics and exceedingly generous backers of the project: Brie Sciales and McCain Moore, James Sciales John and Sylvia Sciales, John and Kate Moran, Luke and Leanne Burns. Your confidence and love humble me.

Hats off to you all, merry patrons. Endless thanks and a warm welcome to what you helped create.

Right, then. On with it. Please, enjoy the stories each for their own.

Pause between them and savor especially those few bizarre pages offered up by a handful of eager artists who volunteered to participate in the miracle.

Drop me a line whenever you'd like to think aloud about something together.

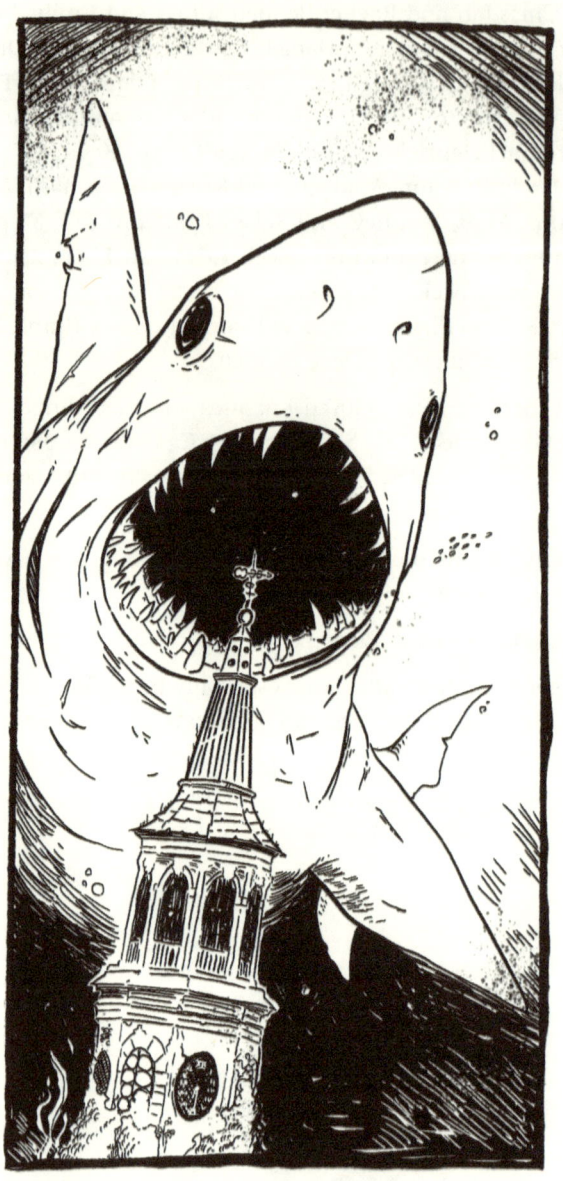

The Stories

The Gray Hand

I've held onto this for over 40 years. Never told a word of it to anyone. Not my wife, my kids, my closest friends. Not once. I'm writing it down here, exactly as I remember it. Maybe it'll clear my conscience, let a decent kid be remembered by someone.

Maybe it won't. In fact, I'm almost sure it won't.

I don't know if writing this down will be the end of me, but I can't hang on to it anymore.

· · ·

Our bus driver, Martin, was a weird dude. Big, hulking guy with chunky jowls. He had this lowbrow stench to him that never changed, like a moldy skin kind of funk. He wore a ratty t-shirt under this patched-up black denim vest, every day. He had big shades, too, reflective, so we couldn't see exactly what he was looking at. Scratched and bent all to hell. Not a charmer, but he didn't give a fuck what we did on that bus. He never looked up.

Well—just when kids got nuts. Not just loud. I'm talking fireworks-going-off, boxing-match nuts. He'd get up, lumber back, sit 'em down on the bench seat, kneel beside them. We'd all kind of hush when this happened. He had that presence. He'd lift his glasses up, look the offending parties dead in the eyes, and just talk to them. Real, real quiet, so no one else could hear.

Whatever he said, it always shut them up. And none of them would talk about it, ever. Like... he cursed them to silence or something. Made them mute. We didn't know. They just wouldn't talk about it.

So that's Martin.

On that last, godawful ride, I dropped into the seat behind Martin, ignoring the smell. I leaned my head on the window, put my pack on the seat next to me, and passed out.

I woke up to my pack getting shoved into my ribs. It hurt. I remember feeling that adolescent spark of outrage; the pain had surprised me. I glare up at the guy, thin and wiry, stark white, scrawny kid. Slipknot shirt. He glares back. He's got short-cropped ultra-black hair. I glance down at my pack, at his translucent hands on it. He's got a spiderweb stretching from his wrist to his knuckles on one hand, with a big black widow, off-center. Not a real tat'— he drew it on with a pen.

Jason. An artist. A loner. I've been riding the same bus as him for years. We live pretty close. He had a little crew of come-and-go misfits he ran with sometimes. I'd overheard him joking around with them plenty. Hit me in a flash when I looked at him. Bragging. Bragging about how independent he was. How he fended for himself. No parents breathing down his neck. Nobody up his ass about college.

That kind of talk can make you jealous, at the right age.

So, I glared at him, he glared back at me, jabbing my books into my ribs. Challenging me to say something, you know? We hung there, suspended in mutual distaste.

"Sit down," Martin barked, and the doors slammed shut. I looked back down the bus. It had packed out. Every seat had two bodies in it, minimum. Jason gave my pack another shove, and I pulled it into my lap with a last scathing look. He sat down next to me.

I laid my head on the window again, fuming in silence and rubbing my bruised ribs with an elbow. I couldn't do much else. Didn't want Martin on my case, didn't want trouble.

Jason, for his part, didn't look at me after he sat.

Good. Great. We didn't have to be friends; we just needed to get home. Whatever.

Between the aching ribs, the smells, and the weirdo, I couldn't fall back to sleep. This was before cell phones, you know? Couldn't just get lost in the screen.

I had a really good view of Martin from where I sat. He looked paler than usual and sweatier, too. I could see his face in the mirror, splotches of red scattered across those pasty jowls. And I could see the back of his neck. Broad. Pale. Greasy locks of hair came halfway down it, brushing against the top of this tattoo that ran across his spine.

The tattoo... Still makes my guy clench to think about it.

It was this shadowy gray hand, but fucked-up looking. Gray, light gray, like dead flesh or thin smoke. And it had these long, wavy fingers and red claws. The whole thing kind of streamed across the back of his neck, the fingers stretching out toward his left shoulder. And the veins. White veins crept across the hand, tapering off like the real thing. Really gross to look at. I couldn't imagine why you'd want it on the back of your neck.

So I noticed the tat', then remembered Jason's hand. Pretty sick art for a younger artist. Good detail and shading. At a glance, you'd have thought the spider could crawl right off his hand. I glanced up at Jason— he had his eyes set on Martin's neck. He caught me looking, turned his head real slow. I froze, chest tight. I'd cooled off a bit during the ride, but Jason was always angry. Always ready for a fight. I was just looking at the guy! My heart pounded. I hadn't gotten used to conflict yet. I was scared, man. I panicked and I shmoozed him. Instinctually, I guess.

"Sick art," I said, nodding down to his hand. He glanced down at it then up to me, a challenge and question. His fingers twitched toward a fist, making the spider dance. He thought I was mocking him. I needed to drive it home. "The uhm... spider. It looks real, bro. Like it could crawl away."

He stared at me for another long second. Then held the hand out, so I could get a better look.

"Not your 'bro'," he said. "And it's a black widow." He had this gently musty, unwashed smell to him. Not terrible, just not what I was used to. I guessed he might dabble in personal hygiene, but didn't have a routine about it. "They operate alone. Even eat each other when they're young."

His eyes softened, offering less of a challenge. A bit less, anyway.

"You want one?" he asked, curt and direct. "I could do something less creepy for you. Maybe a pack animal? Like a wolf or a deer or something? Capybara?"

The pen appeared in his hand out of nowhere. It was a nice one, a sketch artist's pen with a fine tip. He spun it around his finger with a snap. The kid must have lived with that pen in his hand.

"Capy- what?"

"Capybara. Fuzzy brown mammals. They live in herds," he said. "Mostly in South America. You want one? Could even do a herd." He fidgeted with the pen cap and we both looked down at my hand. The blank canvas. Well-scrubbed and prepped for ink.

I thought about how my parents would react. And/or overreact...
"You let a *stranger* draw a *tattoo* on you? What's next? A real tattoo?
Motorcycles? Marijuana? Cocaine? Meth?" Cut to me trying to explain
that capybaras are cute herd animals and that I meant well... Cut to
a lecture on the many dangers of the suburbs. Drugs, alcohol, poor
hygiene, domestic terrorist cells, etc. No Nintendo after dinner.
Straight to bed. And... scene.

"Uhm—nah, nah, I'm good, man," I said. "Looks good on you,
though."

"Well, why the fuck did you say something if you don't want one?"
The pen flipped around and he brandished it like a tiny knife.

"Just thought it looked cool," I said, holding my own hands up a
little. "Just liked the art. No offense." He stared at me. I watched his
knuckles slowly relax around the pen and let my hands lower.

"What do you think of that?" I asked, nodding at Martin's neck.
Jason glanced at it.

"Pretty good," he said. "The way those white veins pop out, that's
cool, but they kind of fuck with the smokey texture. The waviness of it."

"Yeah, sure, the veins could be better," I said. We both looked back
at the tat.

It had switched sides. Those long, wavy fingers stretched out to the
right now. I... know it sounds nuts. I know. And don't worry. It gets
worse. So much worse.

Jason looked at me, wide-eyed.

"You see that shit?" he asked.

"See what?" I played it off. Of course I saw it. I didn't want to see it. I
really didn't. I wanted nothing to do with that slithery hand. Let it be.

"Nahhh, man," he said in a low voice. "Nahhh. Don't fuck with me,
man. You *can't* fuck with me, man—no one can. That shit *moved*!"
His knuckles went white around the pen again and started my heart
pounding. I just wanted to get home.

Jason eyed me again, daring me to disagree. I looked from him to
the tattoo and back, stalling, trying to figure out how to shmooze out
of it. But. The tattoo had moved. Really moved.

"Maybe," I said, "Maybe it did."

He didn't answer. Didn't blink. Didn't breathe. "Maybe" wasn't enough.

"Yeah..." he said, finally, darting a glance at the tattoo, then back to my wide eyes. "Yeahhh. You're gonna ask him about it." Not a question.

I gave him my incredulous brows and let my face twist up with a little *the-fuck-I-am*. But before I could open my mouth, he had the sharp tip of the pen against my neck. I glanced up to the mirror, Martin's bug-eyed lenses pointed straight out the windshield, ignoring us, as usual. The pen pressure disappeared from my neck and reappeared between my ribs.

"Ask where he got that tattoo," Jason growled. "Or I put holes in your lungs."

I glanced down at the hand. The spider. The pen. I got mad. Like. Real mad.

All my stress— you know: tests, classes, couldn't even catch a nap on the damn bus, and now this scrawny little asshole on a power trip. `I just saw red.

Next thing I knew, I've got his pen hand by the wrist and I'm standing over him, just whaling on him with my other fist. I'm no fighter, so I'm barely catching any blows. He's jabbing back, trying to free up the pen, scrappy but too wiry. I heard my shirt tear. We're both getting cuts and bruises all over, grunting and clamoring.

The bus slammed to a stop and we toppled into the aisle, still going after each other.

I felt a sweat-slick, meaty hand grab the back of my neck. Martin wrenched me into the seat, throwing me to the window before he turned to Jason. My ass had barely touched down when I sprang back and went after him again. Nothing could have mattered more than taking a last swing at that prick.

Then, *wham*, Martin snatched me up by the throat, clamping those thick fingers around it. He gripped tight, flexed just a hair to crush my baby Adam's apple. That shocked me into cooling off. I looked up into the sunglasses, saw my own face, blotchy and red, but suddenly wide-eyed with terror. My stomach dropped out. Freefall. It was happening.

It was happening to me. I swallowed; the edge of his hand made it painful. My next breaths came sharp and short.

Martin let me go. He knelt down. The bus had gone completely and totally silent.

He pushed his shades up, trapping his greasy hair back. He had *pitch black* irises. Not, like a dark brown. They were jet, jet black. The rest of his eyes showed a mass of red veins over a sickly yellow. I trembled in my seat. I remember worrying for a split second that Jason would think I was weak for that. But he was quaking, too.

Then Martin's lips moved, but instead of words I heard a shapeless whisper. I stared into those black pits and felt the space around me disappear. Maybe I disappeared. I don't know. It felt real, that I can say for sure.

I was standing outside my house, where I lived with my family. Streetlights were on, moonlight on the fresh cut grass. Night time in my neighborhood. It should have felt safe and familiar, but my blood steamed in my veins. Martin stood in front of me, staring at the house. I could see his shades perched atop his head. The smokey tattoo hand waved like a flag in a light breeze. I hated it.

My parents' silhouettes walked past the front window. I started to cry out.

Martin took one step and I felt a tug in my gut, like I had a harpoon in me and Martin had dragged it behind him. We stood in the living room. My mom's cherished antique furniture all around. My parents stood in front of us by the couch. They were furious, screaming at Martin. Pointing at me. Then at him. I couldn't hear anything, just watched them screeching, gesticulating, all in dead silence. My dad went for the living room phone, jammed three buttons.

Then... the hand on the back of Martin's neck... flexed. It clenched down on his spine and this... shadow monster... crawled up out of Martin's neck.

Using that hand to push and pull and free itself, a demon of swirling black fog emerged. Clouds of shadow boiled up, looming over us. A White veins appeared, pulsing to cast grayish light through the smoke clouds. It coiled around itself, wavy lines of vapor with razor sharp edges. And it had a face. It turned toward me. Two glowing red eyes and a wide mouth with hundreds of short, sharp teeth. Everything about it had a hint of transparency— except the teeth. The teeth glinted in the light. The demon grinned at me.

Shadows flashed. A sudden gush of noise and wind.

The monster exploded out, plunging the room in a cloud of dark smoke. Sound rushed in. Screams. I heard my parents' shrieking. I took a step forward, shouting for them. By the time my foot fell, the smoke had whipped around the room and swirled back into the monster hovering over Martin. The walls were covered in sprays of blood. Four bloody lumps lay on the carpet.

My dad's trainers. My mom's slippers. I saw the bones and flesh of their ankles in the shoes.

"I will know if you speak of me," the thing said. All raspy, like it had a cigarette in its throat.

I snapped back to the bus, gasping, convulsing. I had my arms wrapped around my chest, stomach churning, heart pounding. Martin had already moved over to Jason. I curled up, holding back my vomit. Jason's shaking grew violent, rattling the seat. I cowered, Jason gasped. Martin pulled his shades back down over his black eyes. His mouth turned down in a frown, but softer than usual. He looked at Jason.

Pity. I thought I saw pity.

He reached out and patted the spider on Jason's hand before he stood up.

"You two are my last stops today," he said, low and gravelly. Then he went back to the steering wheel and started driving.

He changed the route. Dropped off every other kid. We sat there shivering, wide-eyed. We couldn't even look at each other. I think Jason prayed. He curled up in the seat and rocked back and forth for a while. I just tried not to cry.

We pulled up at this shopping mall that had gone under, halfway between my neighborhood and Jason's. God, we were shaking. All quiet on the empty bus. Darkness falling outside. The bus teetered into the parking lot, creaking. The brakes squealed; Jason and I jumped. We stuttered to a halt beneath a single streetlight.

Martin stood up, rocking the bus as he turned around. We panted under his stare, though he had his shades down. His head turned from Jason, to me, and back. Jason looked at me, then down at his hands. The spider danced as they shook.

I hate myself for what I said next. It made me sick the moment I said it. Makes me sick now. I've never repeated it, but I remember it word for word. My voice cracked when I started, but it smoothed out as I went.

"I..." I coughed, my bruised throat aching, "I—*hngh*—I got people, man. Family. Friends. People know me. You can't kill half the town, right? They'll come for you. For real." I paused, standing on the brink of the unthinkable. Jason looked empty and hollow. "He's got no one."

Jason started crying. Martin swung his gaze to Jason and left it there.

"You. Up," he rasped. "And out." He left. The bus rocked as his weight left it. Still crying softly, Jason stood up, took his pen, and traipsed off the bus. I just sat there, shivering so hard I almost shit my pants. At first I had my eyes squeezed shut. But. That was too far. I owed it to him. Owed it to Jason to witness. I looked out into the dusk. The world got murky. Jason stopped in front of Martin. A tiny, pale ghost at the foot of a mountain. I stopped breathing. Martin raised his shades again. Then Jason lunged at him with the pen, snarling, screaming.

The gray cloud swept up out of Martin's neck in a flash. Eyes glowed red in the evening gloom, smoke boiled, veins flashed white, teeth glistened. The dark cloud whirled around them and Jason's scream cut short. The smoke froze, unnaturally. Nothing moved, for a moment.

Then the smoke snapped up in the air and drained back into Martin's neck, slowly.

Shoes. A beat-up pair of hightops lay on the ground.

Martin picked them up and tied the laces together. He swung them once, twice, then let them fly up, up. They tangled around a wire overhead— next to the others.

He climbed back on the bus, rocking it again. His smell had changed, all the fat stench from before, but now laced with the sharp scent of blood. His face and sunglasses had dark specks on them. I still had my eyes locked on the row of shoes. Different types and sizes. The streetlight hit something in one of Jason's shoes and I looked closer.

Flesh and ankle bone. I wretched, then vomited my lunch on the floor of the bus.

Martin paused, looked at me.

"If you talk," he said, "they won't believe you. But I'll know."

He tapped his glasses.

I started crying.

Martin sat down and drove me home.

We're Live with Rib!

Chatlin O'Brien sat behind the wood desk of the Late, Late Show. He flipped through the notes from his writers, but he couldn't read them. The world had gone well and truly mad—and the show host found himself at the center of it. He grinned to himself.

"Chatlin!" an assistant producer hissed. He glanced over. She held up a hand. "We're on in FIVE...!" She counted down with silent fingers, and he beamed at the cameras between him and the studio audience. The countdown pumped blood to his hands.

His studio. His time.

"Goooooooood evening, America! Welcome *back* to the Late Late Show! I'm your host, Chatlin O'Brien, and I hope you had a light dinner because tonight is going to be a WILD ride!"

Now, the intro. Normal gaffs on a normal night, as if... as if their guest might *not* be immortal. Chatlin had his doubts.

"First a quick tour of the headlines! Starting with—Congressman Lehigh!"

Audience groans.

"I haven't even started yet, people! Wow. Calm down!"

Laughs. Chatlin let the pause drag for a beat as a picture of Representative Lehigh, wearing his customary jacket and striped tie, popped into view on the monitors. The man had an unbearably square jaw, shaved clean, along with the stoicism of the exquisitely self-righteous. A punchable face; God's gift to comedians.

"Okay. Now. As I was saying. The noble Representative from Missouri has proposed a new bill which will effectively re-criminalize marijuana in America."

Boos.

The image of Lehigh wavered and now he wore a red t-shirt which read "Make America Low Again."

Laughs.

"And that's not all! I have here a list of other policies Congressman Lehigh has proposed."

Chatlin picked up the prop, a scroll of parchment. He gave it a flourish. The roll fell with a satisfying clunk on his desk, then trundled down, unwinding across the stage and halfway over to the band's plat-form. Chatlin feigned shock as the audience laughed.

"Looks like the Representative has something for everyone!" Chatlin shouted, putting on his spectacles and scanning the list. "Alright, let's see here... Oh, now that's— *I* haven't even gotten to try half of these things." Laughs. "Tell you what— Hey, Tony?"

"Yeah?!" The guitarist leaned over to speak into his mic.

"I think I need some more—experienced folks to help me out here." Small laughs. "Why don't you ask about some of your hobbies so we can see if you'd get jail time in Representative Lehigh's Fourth Reich of Missouri."

Laughs.

"Alright, Chatlin, alright. So, no marijuana, right?"

"Correct. Outlawed."

"Well, can we drink?"

"Uhmmm, oh! YES! Well, no. Does nine to midnight on weekends count?"

"HELL no!"

A *womp womp* from the tuba.

Laughs

The bandmates rattled them off, and Chatlin responded.

Mushrooms? No. Plan B? No. Cigarettes? No.

Kissing in public?! Nein!

Nein nein nein! No!

The band conferred.

"Well, that's it, folks. I think that's everything fun. The safest thing to do—"

"Wait!" Tony shouted. "Wait!"

A long pause.

"What about blow jobs?!"

Laughs.

"Annnnd cunnilingus?!" shouted the saxophonist, tossing her hair. A lilting cheers from the audience.

Chatlin scanned the scroll.

"Uhm—"

Paper riffled across his desk as he pulled it hand over hand.

"Uhm. Uhm. Uhmmm... Wait a minute folks!"

Chatlin leaped up, and the band played him a racy little tune as he tramped around, examining various sections of the parchment. He dragged the bit out, clung to it, nearly strangled the life out of it.

When the tension waned too much, he snatched up the scroll and waved it overhead.

"Oral sex is safe!"

The audience cheered uproariously with no cue.

Normal gaffs, normal laughs.

Chatlin made his way back behind the desk. Stagehands scurried out and grabbed the scroll, bundling it up, dropping it, and tripping over it. A few last chuckles eked out as they made it disappear backstage.

He pretended to organize his note cards while the crowd's laughter guttered out. He glanced backstage. The producer arched an eyebrow and motioned for him to pick up the pace. With practiced grace, he brought in a steadying breath, soft enough that the mic wouldn't catch it.

"Now," he said, in his important-things-are-happening voice, "enough about the big wide world. Tonight's guest is QUITE the polarizing figure. Please, help me welcome to the stage, Ribald' The Rib' Egresssssss!!! The INDESTRUCTIBLE MAN!!!"

Muted cheers and boos mingled in the audience. Chatlin swallowed his shock. They always cheered for the guest. Always.

A screech of metal came from stage left. Chatlin watched the entire curtain ensemble, a thousand pounds of velvet and metal, crumple to the ground. The audience gasped, uncued. A grunt, a heave, and he emerged. "The Rib" dragged the clanking mass up his massive back and tied two corners of the curtain around his neck. A cape. He'd made a cape.

Backstage, the exposed stagehands scattered from the bright lights, limbs flailing. They fumbled over one another, scrambling to drag props out of sight. Laughs, boos, and cheers raced through the audience. One of the hands tripped on the "cape" and threw up their hands. Rib caught them by the back of the shirt, pulled them upright, and scooted them along. Chatlin made a note to commend the hands for stellar improvisation. He laughed and clapped along with the audience, letting Rib's grand entrance own the limelight for a few beats.

The man wore a tank top, tight buzz cut, and cargo shorts. He'd bronzed his pale skin and whitened his teeth to rival Chatlin's. They gleamed as he lifted two massive arms overhead and laughed with the crowd. A small gold earring, a simple letter "M," glittered on one of his ears.

"MURDERER!" someone shouted from the stands. Chatlin froze for a moment, terror clutching at his heart. But Rib just flipped his heckler the bird with a big grin. Easy to censor. No harm, no foul.

"Alright, alright, easy now!" Chatlin shouted, laughing it off. Bouncers dragged the heckler out. Relief surged. "Welcome, Rib! Welcome! Have a seat!" The big man turned his brilliant smile to Chatlin. It was warm. Genuinely warm, all the way up to the eyes and back. Interview enough people on camera and you learn to see the soul in a split second. This man had no qualms about his life or choices, none whatsoever. So rare.

Still chuckling, Rib tugged the "cape" off and cast it aside. Chatlin watched his hand disappear into the cavern of Rib's paw. He gave it an astonished look, for the audience. Rib gave his hand the lightest squeeze. Perfect self-possession. And the smile. Chatlin's smile had dragged him through two dozen rocky years of show business. This barrel-chested meathead could almost outshine him.

Rib sat. The ample chair groaned, and the big man made a scared face, holding his hands out. The audience laughed. No one booed. His humility drew them in.

"What an INCREDIBLE honor it is for you to have me on the show!" Rib shouted at Chatlin. "Sorry about the curtain! I just love to make an entrance." He smiled and laughed, and the audience joined along. Chatlin went with it.

"I know, of all the silly late-night variety shows, you chose to wreck ours," Chatlin said, grinning too hard. The audience laughed on cue. "We're so flattered."

Chatlin fanned himself with his note cards, then tapped them on the desk, smiling as the laughs trailed off. He needed to get them back on script. The man was good. And a loose cannon.

"So. Why us, Rib?"

"2.2 million!" Rib boomed, leaning back in his chair. "I had 2.2 million and one good reason, Chatty BOY!"

Word-perfect to what they'd agreed on. Chatlin relaxed into the comic pause... Then shot a frightened look at Camera One.

"Wait! We're not *paying* you to be here, are we?"

"No way, brother!" Rib smiled and slapped the arm of the chair. "Why? Are they paying you?!" He had a brazen way of speaking, like someone at the back might not hear him. Someone at the back whose life he could change with a word. Someone who should be scared—no, *terrified*—to miss out.

The audience laughed again. More of them than before. The boos were swaying, waffling.

"Okay, okay, so 2.2 million and one reasons—" Chatlin prompted.

"Right, well, the Late, Late Show has one *million* BADASS viewers!!!" Rib gestured to the audience, and they cheered for themselves. "Annnnd... don't take this the wrong way, Chat, but the Rib Lovers crew is 1.2 million strong and counting!!!"

Half the crowd roared. Some booed. Chatlin nodded good-naturedly.

"Yes, yes, quite the following! And zero overlap between our audiences! Can't *imagine* why that would be..." Theatrical eye roll. Laughter from the crowd. "You said 2.2 million and one. So, who or what is the other *one*?" Chatlin gave him the old eyebrow waggle.

Rib grinned at him, again with a surge of warmth, then swatted the air with a bashful wave.

"Oh, you know it's you, Chat! Huge fan of the show! I came here just to share some of my darkest..." he trailed off, and the audience hushed. A natural crowd-herder. "Secrets."

Intrigued murmurs from the audience

"Oh yeah?!" Chatlin demanded, with a big grin for the cameras, "And you're gonna be *totally, completely* honest?!"

"I always am, Chat."

"Okay... okay..." said Chatlin, pretending to think. "Welllll, now. I have to ask the obvious question: Are you *really* indestructible?"

Serious look. Long pause. Longer. Longer still. The audience hung on the hook. Then, BAM! The big grin, arms wide.

"Of course!" Rib shouted. Massive flex of the arms overhead, bear-like. The audience roared, drowning out the boos. Chatlin still only half-believed. He didn't want to.

"Oh?! And how does one find out that one's invincible? Some sort of test? A trial of the gods?"

"Well, it's a lonnnnnng story, actually," Rib said.

"Well, it's a short show," Chatlin grinned and rolled a finger at Rib. "So, chop-chop, big man."

"Hah!" Rib shouted, laughing along with the crowd. "Fine! The short version! So... I had 400 pounds on the bench, right? Camera on for my 20,000 OG followers!!" Rib paused to flex his pecs and grin, listening to the cheers. He lifted an imaginary bar. "Dropped it right on my *throat!!! Acchhh!*" He acted out the scene with choking noises; laughter cascaded down the stands.

"And...?"

"Not a mark!" Rib said, showing his unblemished neck.

"Wow!" remarked Chatlin with a grin for Camera Two. "UN-believable!"

"That's what I said. 'Wow.' So they ran some tests and told me some things... We'll skip the whole origin story since this is the short version."

"Thanks."

"Eventually, I had that misunderstanding at the bank..." Boos and cheers. "I know, I know!" Hands raised. "Listen, I had my reasons for going down there. And I never meant for those officers to be hurt." He paused, somber, for effect, lowering his hands, bringing the energy of the room down with them. Boos echoed in the absence of laughter.

"An unfortunate incident..." Chatlin added, hedging.

"Truly. Broke my heart. And people thought I staged the whole thing..." He shook his head, letting his gaze slide down and out. Then the grin came back, and he snapped back to Camera One. "So! I came here tonight to play a game."

He reached behind him. Then, *clunk*, a handgun landed on Chatlin's desk.

It was supposed to be a bat. Or a tire iron, at worst. Something slapstick. This. This was—unscripted. Live television. The host threw his hands up. Just another prop, another gaff. The audience laughed, but Rib carefully turned the gun barrel to point at himself.

The producer waved a question, *Go off air?!* But Chatlin didn't dare. Below his desk, he rolled his finger to keep the cameras live. Rib caught the motion and grinned at him.

The big man leaned over, his chair creaking in the now silent studio, and pushed the handgun across the desk. It bumped Chatlin's fingertips.

"Pick it up," Rib said. "Then wait."

Numb, Chatlin picked up the weapon. The metal felt cold and heavy in his hand, a real gun. Terror ran through him. He smiled, as always.

"Now," Rib said, "before we play. Two rules. So we don't have any misunderstandings. First rule, the cameras roll, no matter what." He smiled out at the audience and the lenses. "Second, tell the truth."

He paused. Chatlin glanced past him. The band had slipped away, their abandoned drums, brass, and guitars sparkled in the set lights.

"Agreed?" The joy and mischief had slipped away. Chatlin thought he saw something cold and straightforward, but the bit had gone too far to call off.

"Agreed," the host said, letting an unworried smile blaze for the audience.

"So. First question. Do they pay you to be here?"

Chatlin gave a big stage laugh. A few reluctant chuffs came from the audience. Terror had squeezed out fear, but they couldn't look away.

"Of course!" Chatlin said, beaming. "I've gotta eat! Just not as much as you!" A few more laughs.

"Oh, sure!" Rib laughed. "Man's gotta eat! Gotta bulk up!" He slapped an arm and flexed. The audience cheered. "Where's the rest of that money go though, Chatlin? To charity?"

"No, not all of it," Chatlin said, grinning for the crowd. They chuckled.

"You invest most of it," Rib said. "Don't you?" Chatlin looked back at him. The warmth had bled away. Rib looked cold. Hard. "You invest in companies. Buy stocks?"

"Sure! I mean, I don't know where every dollar... goes. But my accountants assure me that it's well cared for." Chatlin stammered.

Rib nodded.

"Of course not, but I bet you know the gist."

"I—"

"For example: You are a primary investor in Blue Heart Insurance, true or false?"

"I—uhm. Yes. I am. True." *Where is this going?*

"You're sure?"

"Of course. It's a good company with good values. 'Helping people heal,' you know?"

He smiled out at the audience and collected a smattering of applause.

"'Helping people heal'," Rib repeated. "That's their slogan, isn't it?" The smile had gone. Hushed whispers ran through the audience. Chatlin glanced at the producer. They looked pale and wide-eyed.

"You're aware of their quarterly reports over the last 7 years then?"

"Well. I'm not a very active—"

"Up and to the right, Chat," Rib said, pointing. "Up and to the right for *seven straight years!* SEVEN!"

The shout made Chatlin jump in his chair. He grinned and put a hand to his chest, hiding his fury.

"You don't find that kind of stock every day," Rib went on. "Must have made you a fortune. How does a company keep up that kind of growth, do you think?"

"Excellent management?" Chatlin quipped, smiling and signaling for a laugh cue with his hidden hand.

Silence.

Chatlin could just see the audience cue screen in the corner of an eye, the word *LAUGH* flashing there, over and over. His blood felt cold in his veins.

"They don't exactly invite me to the board meetings. But I assu—"

"Don't worry," Rib cut in, holding up a hand. "We took a look and crunched the numbers for you. The answer is actually simple."

He paused, eyes hard and leveled on Chatlin now.

"Claim denials."

"Oh, now, hold on—"

"Blue Heart Insurance stopped paying out on claims. Denials spiked seven years ago and rose steady as the sunrise every quarter. Just like your savings."

Chatlin bolted his smile on and scanned the audience. Hard looks from every face. He could almost hear the bleachers creaking as would-be hecklers moved toward the edges of their seat.

"Well, if that's true, and I don't know if it is—"

"Of course you don't," Rib said. "But that's not the point. We do. We know." He turned and spoke to the crowd. "In the last 3 years, Blue Heart denied tens of thousands of legitimate claims. Probably for some of you in this room."

Murmurs now through the audience, skimming over their rapt silence.

"This company buried their own claimants in paperwork until they gave up, ran out of money, or died."

He let that hang in the air. The producer had frozen. Chatlin had nothing to say.

"Now. My Baby Back Crew did some special ops recon. Turns out, Blue Heart Insurance targeted individuals who would die without care. Individuals who would die before they could appeal their claims or fight a prolonged court battle."

Rib reached up and touched his earring.

Rippling whispers flickered over the audience. Chatlin caught fragments. "Let them die." "Good as killed them." "Murder."

Murder.

"Do it, Rib!" someone shouted. Chatlin sat frozen.

Rib's voice rang out.

"Chatlin O'Brien, a primary investor in the Blue Heart Insurance conglomerate, hereby stands accused of murder in the first degree." He raised his fist and slammed it to the desk, crunching the wood. Chatlin stared down at the crater it left. The fist raised, pointer finger aimed at Chatlin's forehead.

"This is your judgment day," Rib said.

The audience held its breath.

Rib let out a sudden, booming laugh, rattling the silent studio. He leaned back in his chair and smiled, jovial and complacent. Chatlin's stomach had flipped, but he tried to laugh along.

Rib smiled to outshine the stage lights.

"Enough melodrama!" he said, jovial as he'd been coming onto stage in his cape. "Let's play the game! Chatlin, be a dear and shoot me in the head. If I die, you live. If I live, then you die."

He paused. All the blood ran out of Chatlin's hands and feet. Numbness crept into his chest.

"Oh! And, please! No one call the police. Or leave the studio. I don't want anyone getting hurt. And keep those cameras rolling!" Rib grinned. "Wouldn't want our 2.2 million friends missing this historic moment."

The audience ruffled. Some stood and were yanked back down. Whispers floated through the crowd. Chatlin only heard one word.

Murder.

"Don't do this, Rib!" someone shouted from the audience.

"You don't have to do this!"

"Let him go!"

"You'll just be one of them!"

Scuffles broke out, cries of pain. Rib reached out, so gently, and pulled the gun from Chatlin's hand. He fired into the air.

BLAM. BLAM. Chatlin jumped twice.

"SIT. DOWN." They sat. "Thank you."

Rib placed the gun back in Chatlin's hand.

So heavy. Grip rough on soft-palms, slick with sweat.

"It's okay," Rib said. "You can do it. And—aim carefully. We don't want another bank incident."

Chatlin exhaled. He prayed. He lifted the gun.

"Well, y-you're the guest," Chatlin said, fighting the chatter of his teeth. He sighted down the barrel, looking into Rib's eyes.

He saw no hesitation, no doubts from The Invincible Man.

He pulled the trigger. The gun leaped in his hand, and the blast made him cry out, ears ringing. Despite that, his eye caught the split-second when the bullet crumpled against Rib's forehead, sending a ripple out across the flesh. The man didn't even blink.

Chatlin put the gun down on the desk. He stared down at the desktop.

Eyes flat, Rib picked the squashed bullet up out of his lap. He showed it to the audience, holding it up by his unmarked forehead. He placed it on the desk with a click and then stood up.

He glowered into Camera 2 and lowered his voice.

"I will kill every primary investor of Blue Heart Insurance, one by one, until they reinstate themselves as a non-profit that serves the people."

The audience cheered—all of them. Rib turned to Chatlin.

"Please..." Chatlin whined. "I didn't know."

His voice sounded small and feeble. He wished he could stop. The indestructible man leaned over Chatlin's desk, massive hands reaching out for his neck.

"Please... I didn't know—I didn't know! I didn't. I didn't. I didn't..."

Riding Kartheros

My lightning harvester shook in my hands. Then it rattled. Shaking is normal. Rattling is bad. Very bad. The gunwale cleats were loose, and the storage fuses were overheating.

Number rolls on the capture register flipped up in a dizzying blur, 5,000 and counting. A standard harvester topped out at 4,000, but Captain Layla Nefferson's designs could hold more.

Too much power, too fast. I could feel the harvester's heat through my thick gloves. It pulsed up to warm my nose and mouth below, fogging my goggles. Clouds whispered past and evaporated as they kissed the hot metal casing. It was overloading. I slid my thumb over the kill switch. I could take the heat.

I could hold on just a little longer.

Show them what I was made of.

Overhead, a concentric ring of bright blue light rippled through the storm. It pulled the *Sheila's* lightrails skyward and filled our lightning nets with crackling charge. We swept and dove through Kartheros, the Endless Storm. Hundreds of feet beneath our hull, Faros, the Endless Sea, heaved and crashed in perpetual torment.

Sparkling ripples zipped out toward the edges of the net above me, sliding around gaps like water over glass. The bolt was nearly spent. I thought I could make it.

The harvester gave another fierce jump in my hands. Then another. The cleats rattled. A gust of wind slapped us with a curtain of water, throwing up clouds of steam all along the gunwales. I heard a scream. My thumb began to press down on the kill switch.

The harvester's moorings snapped.

It went wild, bucking and snapping like a wounded animal. I clutched it toward me and forced it back down to the gunwale, pinning it with my body. *Kill-switch! Kill it!* I couldn't reach it; it was all I could do to restrain it. If I didn't let go, it would explode in my chest. But if I let it fly, it would shoot out to the end of its line, then snap back to the boat and probably kill one of my crewmates. Heat and buzzing electricity burned through my coat.

I was screaming, I realized. Not words. I'd started with a stream of curses and descended into something guttural and desperate. Defiant.

I clung to the harvester, burning, eyes wrenched shut, praying for the lightning to stop.

I felt a hand on my shoulder and snapped my eyes open. My goggles had cleared. The harvester had cooled. Silas stood over me. Silas the Mute. Silence, to the crew. The angled lumps of his many-pocketed coat brushed my chest as he pressed close, mouth sour.

The bulky Mech Lead thrust a fistful of something under my nose. I smelled burnt rubber—the ends of my harvester's cables. He had pulled the cords, broken the circuit. Probably saved my life.

He slapped the harvester, held up a hand to show five fingers, then shut and opened it again to show another two. The stubby digits shook with rage. I'd gone to seven thousand kilos. I should be dead, along with the two hands next to me. Silence held the hand high and flashed the numbers for all the hands to see. *Seven thousand.* Disgusted glares from along the gunwale forced my eyes down.

"I'm sorry–" I started. Silence's hand moved in a flash. He jabbed two fingers up under my chin, pushing me up painfully and holding me there. The grease on them slid on my damp skin. He dropped my harvester cable and picked another, thicker one. He pointed up the mainmast to the crow's nest, mimed plugging in the cord, pointed at his eyes, then over the bow, then back to the stern, and finally tapped his chest twice, hard. *Crow's nest, run this line, check storm cell, report to the wheel. Double-time.*

I dropped the harvester, snatched the thin cable, and ran to the mast. Thunder grumbled in the distance. I checked the cord to make sure it had slack and found plenty. I tied it over my shoulder like the privateers wore their bandoliers. Then my gloves slapped the sodden rope ladder, and I flew up the mainmast, leaving the deck far below.

A blast of lightning whited out the metal net overhead, blowing out my vision. I squinched my eyes shut, but my hands didn't slow on the ladder. Still blind, I flipped over the edge of the crow's nest and took a breath while my eyes recovered. I wrapped one arm in the base of the safety line on the main mast, not bothering to clip in.

The nets crackled hot and heavy overhead. Shouts came from below, the harvesters struggling to keep up with the fury. A squat, faceted metal dome sat on fresh wood in the crow's nest. It was bolted in place and had an empty port. I'd been up to the crow's nest that morning, and the dome hadn't been there. The mystery didn't trouble me. The Captain never shared her plans. Untying the cord from my shoulder, I snugged the end of it into the dome. The chunk of metal gave a tiny whirr.

I popped my head up above the edge of the nest.

We'd flown deep into the storm and high into its strongest cells. Our starboard bow had grazed a triumphant storm cell, the darkening clouds staving us off. To the port side, another cell coiled around itself—furious but manageable. Dead ahead, cloud banks convulsed as they rose and bloomed.

A sudden charge in the air raised every hair on my neck. I glanced to starboard and saw the massive storm cell blossom our way, reaching a club-like paw of wind, rain, and swirling cloud at *Sheila*. I spun toward the stern and stuck my head over the edge of the railing.

"BRACE!" I shrieked down. "TO PORT! ALDRED! HARD TO—"

The wind ripped my voice from my lungs, and a crack of lightning lit the net overhead. The lift of the rails pinned me to the nest, then we peaked, and a gust wormed itself under my body. I screamed as the wind ripped me from the crow's nest.

The safety line caught me, squeezing my arm tight. I hung suspended on the line, terrified, forty feet above the ship, perpendicular to the deck. The gust had buffeted *Sheila's* keel over. From where I swung, I could see her fins jutting out.

A sudden sense of wonder gripped me. Terror slipped away, chased off by an onslaught of giddiness. I giggled at our audacity. Our immeasurable smallness, tickling the heart of this mighty power. I reveled in our resilience, despite its violence. The keel regained itself, fins slipping back under the ship as she righted. Someone had the wheel. The brutal gust subsided. I fell swift and sudden toward the mast, my soaked coat slapped against it, pounding my shoulder into the wood.

The storm cell grumbled at us while I hung there. Another bolt would come—I felt it coiling in the depths of that cloudbank. The bolt, and then the lift. The deck swayed below me, far below. I grinned.

The lightning crackled. I hauled my weight up to get slack in the safety line, then whipped my arm in a circle to unwind it. The flash came, and *Sheila* rode it up.

I slapped down at the rail of the crow's nest and flew up toward the charged lightning net. The safety rope whizzed and rippled through my loose fingers, warming my thick calluses through my gloves. The ship fell away beneath me. When I felt the immense heat and crackling charge of the net, I whipped my arm around, snatching the rope. Beads of water snapped off the line as it tautened.

My arm wrenched painfully as I snapped down toward the deck. Teeth clenched, I blasted through the rain and wind. Fast. Far too fast. The stern raced up to meet me. I felt a sudden, doubting panic.

The line jerked taut again, and my legs swung beneath me. I pulled up my feet as they swept past the startled, ducking heads of the sailors working harvesters along the portside gunwale. Shouted curses followed me to the stairs of the poop deck. I started to lift again. The stern fell away, and I saw the end of the deck—the beginning of a long fall into Faros's jaws.

I let go of the rope. Momentum carried me up, gloriously up, toward the flash of lightning. My foot clipped the top stair and I crashed to the deck .

I laughed, shaking with it as I stood. My blood felt thin and ghostly in my veins, which vibrated like overcharged harvester lines. I clasped my hands together and tried to still them as if I could clamp them down on the laughter wracking my frame. It felt wrong, I knew it to be wrong, but I couldn't stop it. I looked to the wheel, to Aldred.

He stared ahead, hands rigid on the wheel, arms twitching to keep the keel fins steady, to hold the Captain's course.

His lips moved, forming words in clips and phrases. *Storm wall — heart of the storm — Yantes, preserve us — guide us through shadow — walls of Kartheros — heart of the storm.*

Storm mad. Seeing him frozen cut my laughter short. My hands steadied. My blood quieted. My feet felt firm on the deck again.

I stepped up and punched Aldred in the lower back, just beside the spine. May as well have punched a coat hung on a palm tree. His lips didn't slow, and his gaze didn't break.

"Aldred! ALDRED!" I punched him a few more times. He ignored me, clenching the wheel like a day-old corpse.

Lightning flashed, *Sheila* rose, sailors cursed, thunder roared. Water dripped across his goggles. Aldred didn't blink. The ship rocked hard to port. I stepped back, waited for the roll, then strode into it and front-kicked him in his ribs. He broke, stumbling from the wheel and collapsing to the deck. I snapped up the wheel before it could spin free.

He hunched over, breathing. Clutching his rib.

I waited, hoping.

Aldred stood and gently took the wheel back from me, hands light. I exhaled as I stepped back.

"Report, Harken!" he blurted.

"Aye, sir! Massive cell to the starboard side! Storm wall like I've never seen!" I shouted up at him. He nodded along. "Aggressive cloud activity ahead suggests weakness in the cell's wall in the next 2 miles. Skirt this front to port, then cut in at the first opportunity. Not too far to port though! The cell on the port bow looks half as bad."

He nodded.

"Captain wants you below. Send Silence up to me."

"Sir!" I made for the stairs. *Sheila* swayed beneath me, groaning like a burnt sailor on the surgeon's table. The crew looked haggard, fighting their bucking harvesters, frantically swapping fuses. We must have captured two journey's worth of lightning already. In the shouts and wind, I gathered that we'd nearly run through our storage canisters. *Sheila* couldn't hold much more lightning. I caught some scowls from those whose heads I'd nearly clipped. Mostly, they ignored me, as was their way with green sailors.

I found Silence hunkered over my busted harvester, prying free a charred fuse. I rapped his shoulder, hard. He spun and stood. Not smooth, like stacks of wet rock clacking over one another. He glared at me through his thick goggles.

I pointed at him, then jabbed a finger up to Aldred.

"Poop deck!" He scowled. "Aldred's orders!" I tapped my chest twice, *Double time!* Then made a rude gesture. He bristled, but I skipped away toward the nearby hatch. Silence shuffled off, head twitching with unuttered curses. Smiling, I pulled the hatch down over my head, muffling the sounds of wind and rain. Another nasty gust bumped us, and we listed to port.

Sheila swung back under my feet as my boots splashed into the puddle at the bottom of the stairs.

The Captain hunched over her workbench, the hooked arch of her dark neck hinting at her ungainly height. Years of tinkering in her cramped shop aboard the *Sheila* gave her the winding, sinuous posture of a wading heron.

"Harken, reporting."

She snapped a hand up, and I froze mid-step.

"Wait."

Frowning, I planted my feet on a dry spot, unbuttoning my coat and lifting my goggles. The room came alive.

The fabric on her workbench gave a phosphorescent shimmer. The bare bulb overhead tossed blue luminescence over it while the warm glow of the heater above her work table cast it in ambers. Both lights fractured on the fabric, and a thousand colors cascaded over the tool racks lining the timber walls. It smelled of grease and old, damp wood. I should have seen the beauty in it, but I just felt sick to my stomach.

The Captain's spidery, brown fingers skittered over sheets of shimmering fabric and metal flotsam. She swayed in time with the ship, viciously snapping and twitching the material on the bench. The chaos seemed to have some rhythm to it, and she hummed as the mysterious contraption took shape beneath her. It appeared to have wings and horns. I swallowed.

"Twin bitches, Layla and *Sheila*, made for one another in the depths of Hell," the sailors in port said. "Fed more good hands to Faros than all the rest of these schooners together."

I hadn't listened.

More fool me.

A boom sounded from without. I felt *Sheila's* sharp lift, then heard the shriek of metal and a loud groan from the hull. In the relative quiet, I heard the tiny crackling sounds of wood beams pulling apart. I winced.

Captain Layla Nefferson, the Bent Nail, didn't flinch. Without glancing up from the fabric, she tossed a scalpel toward a rack of tools. The charged rack snicked the handle from the air, securing it in line. She snatched up a pair of pliers and began a repetitive motion. On her hip, the polished wood handle of her long-barreled lightning pistol glinted in the lights.

Notes and sketches fluttered on the wall above her workbench. She'd tacked up line after line of equations and dimensions. Drawings of wings and limbs. One half-page sketch, in the water-stained top right corner, looked like a horned fruit bat.

"Heard a harvester overload," the Captain said, snatching my attention. "Yours?"

"No."

A spidery hand flicked up, pliers returned, *snick*, pipe wrench out, *click*. She hefted the heavy tool once, then whipped her arm backward. It flew straight for my windpipe. I flinched away, but it cracked into my sore shoulder. I cried out at the jolt of pain. The wrench clattered to the floor.

"Bring that back."

I glared at her back. Picked up the wrench. Without thinking, I lifted it up over my head as if to smash it down on the puff of white hair springing up from her goggle strap. Her head turned minutely, one eye flashing up to the wrench. She smirked.

"Place it there." She nodded to an empty corner of the bench.

I put the wrench down, trying and failing to keep the rage from my face. She already had the pliers out and moving again, planting bright rivets along a seam. I stepped back, rubbing my shoulder.

"Never lie to me," she said.

I didn't reply. She worked the rivets.

Another wretched creak came from the hull.

"Easy, girl," the Captain cooed. Not to me. "Almost ready."

"Captain—"

"Wait."

I waited, shoulder throbbing, sweat beading under my coat. Tools glistened. Fabric rustled. Spider-fingers stitched and plied and snapped. We lifted and fell, lifted and fell. The hull shuddered, then creaked.

Louder.

Louder.

The deck rolled hard to port. The Captain muttered a small curse and gave her feet a deft twitch to catch herself. Her head never wavered. The whole ship seemed to rotate around her. I glanced down at my own waxen pants and scuffed boots as my feet mimicked hers.

We both anticipated the counter-roll. Instead, *Sheila* lurched beneath us, and we stumbled.

A slam from overhead and a sudden roar of the wind. A sluice of rainwater splashed down the steps, joining the puddle at the base.

Heavy steps clomped down the stairs and Aldred appeared, ripping his goggles up and slapping a hand on the bulkhead as he crashed to a stop at the foot of the stairs.

"Captain!" he shouted down the last few steps, his bushy beard dripping. "The foresail's got a yard-long tear in her already, and the crew's scared half to mutiny!"

"They can wait," she said. "You can all wait..."

The Captain snapped home another rivet. Another.

Aldred's jaw worked noiselessly. Then he stepped up beside me and clasped his hands behind his back. I snuck glances at him while the Captain worked. Mutters of an old prayer slipped through his beard bristles.

Yantes, Mother—burn eternal—eyes from darkness—Guide us.

His eyes showed veiny white at the edges. I looked away.

snap

snap

creak

snap

snap

The ship lurched. Metal screeched. More curses above. Aldred winced, then took a large breath and straightened his shoulders, opening his mouth.

"Speak!" the Captain said. Aldred blinked.

"Captain! We've maintained your heading as long as we can."

"I very much doubt that." The scorn in her salted rasp bit deep.

"Captain, please! She's coming apart. Can't you hear her?! We can't—"

"We can and we will," she said.

"Captain," I said, "I saw the storm wall with my own eyes. It's—I saw it—uhm—"

A handful of words hit my throat at the same time, none of them sane. Only a choked sound slipped out.

The Captain set her work down and turned around. The leather strap of her green lenses barely held back her wild white hair. She smiled at us like we were petulant children begging for a bedtime story. The bitch.

"It nearly killed her, Captain," Aldred said. "Nearly drove her mad."

The Bent Nail's round eyes slid to me. Aldred babbled.

"Leap out of the crow's nest like a storm-addled lunatic, laughing like a gull. It'll kill all of us. We're in too deep, too close to his heart. He won't let us go without—" Aldred swallowed. "We have a king's harvest worth o' lightning; no schooner could ask for more. If we turn back now, maybe we can..."

He trailed off.

"You were in the nest, Harken?" she asked. She grinned at me now, mocking, almost leering, showing her yellow teeth. I clenched my teeth shut.

Yes.

"What did you see?"

A storm front. The fist of a god.

"And what did you feel?"

Inconceivable power.

"And—most importantly—what did you do next?"

I pictured the rope pulling taut, the sweep of my fall from the crow's nest. Letting go of the rope and flying. Laughing. A laughing fit to raise a drowned man up from Faros.

She grinned at me. Six hardy sailors couldn't have pried my mouth open with a crowbar.

"She read the storm. Well as I could or better," Aldred said, the great betrayer. "Then she damn near killed herself swinging down from the crow's nest. And her less than a year on ship. Then she—"

I lashed out and smashed his shin with my boot.

"Nnnngghhh," Aldred gurgled. "Then she kicked some sense into me."

"Did she now?" her grin flashed to Aldred, then faded at the look on his face.

"Captain, please—"

A sharp tug drew us all up, and a loud splintering came from the center beam of the hull. We froze. A crack formed, and water beaded along the beam, quivering.

A frown twisted the Captain's lips. She took a long step to a gap in the tools where the rough wood of Layla's hull stood exposed. Pressing her palm to the timber, she closed her eyes. My heart dropped into my stomach, and I nearly prayed.

Water beaded up between her thin fingers. Aldred tensed and leaned in as if to speak, but I reached over to grab his arm.

The Bent Nail began to hum and tap her foot.

We stared at her and listened.

She hummed, the wind howled, and the thunder rolled clever circles all around us. The Captain harmonized... with the Storm. She sang along with the madness of Kartheros.

"I left Silence with orders to veer forty degrees to port if he sees an opening," Aldred said, brushing my hand off. "We have to pull back, Silence agrees—"

The Captain's hand snapped to her hip. A flash of blue light and a sharp *crack* filled the cabin. Aldred collapsed to the deck, screaming and holding his leg. Smoke rose from his thigh in a lazy trickle, a mirror to the tendril rising from the Captain's gun. The metallic scent of electricity mingled with the sourness of burning flesh.

Aldred's hand went to his own pistol, but the Captain thumbed back her hammer without looking down. Her eyes remained closed. I took a step and put my foot on Aldred's wrist before he could draw. He couldn't pull his eyes from the barrel of her gun.

"Don't move," she said softly. "Don't speak."

With her hand on the hull wall and her pistol aimed at Aldred, the Bent Nail swayed with the ship.

The ship swayed, but the bead of the pistol kept steady on Aldred. I held my foot on his wrist. Drops of blood trickled from his leg. It wouldn't bleed much, lightning-shot cauterizes. The drops disappeared into the rivulets of water on the deck.

The Captain began to hum, a low, haunting tune, rising and falling. Then I heard the wind. She harmonized with it again. More than matching the song, she anticipated it, then wallowed and soared with it.

The hull shuddered again, and it sent an echoing shiver down the Captain's arm. It trembled up her neck to the tip of her nose and then down the bony rails of her frame, flicking her coattails.

Her eyes flipped open.

She holstered the pistol and patted *Sheila's* cracked beam, then went to the workbench and gathered up her project.

"Harken, help Aldred up to the wheel," she snapped.

Then she splashed through the puddle and up the stairs. She slammed the top hatch open, orders for the sailors above deck ripping from her throat before she'd left the hold.

Aldred and I breathed together in the quiet workshop. I took my foot from his wrist. The sudden urge to cry clamored at my throat, but I pushed it down. Aldred touched the hole burnt in his pants and moaned.

I found some thick straps of leather on the wall and a jar of burn ointment. With his goggles up, I could see the tight, pale skin around Aldred's eyes. He worked his jaw in silence while I bound the wound.

The shake in my hands slowed me.

"Why're you here, Hark?"

I worked the leather without answering.

"She'll kill me soon, you know."

My hands froze for an instant.

"Not many sailors left who're crazy enough to run with her," I said, forcing my voice toward calmness. I continued to wrap the leg. "And none she'd suffer as a mate. She needs you."

He started to shake his head, but I cinched the knot. Hard. He gasped, then let the pain out through clenched teeth. His eyes snapped to mine, a little too wide, then they wandered up, toward the bridge.

"We'll see..."

Sneaking my frame under his large arm, I helped him slide up the wall. A grunt slipped through his beard when he put weight on his wounded leg, but he didn't falter. We stood there together, staring at the stairs while the ship swayed. We leaned into the tug as she turned.

To starboard. *Deeper.*

"Yantes, hear our prayers," Aldred whispered.

He took the first step and I fell in. We worked up the stairs in a pitiful series of hops and grunts. A pause before the hatch. *Goggles on, ears in.* I cracked open the wood and iron. Kartheros ripped it open, groping for us, wind rattling the tools below. Aldred dragged himself into the wind; I followed, then fought the hatch shut.

Thick mists swarmed the decks, endless torrents ripping past. Crewmen appeared from the ether, then were swallowed whole as we made our way aft, stumbling and sliding on the deck. A sudden ring of lightning sparked directly above the *Sheila.* The crack of thunder rang my ears through the dampeners, thudding inside my chest. Impossibly loud and close.

The lift came sudden and brutal, making our torsos heavy on our legs. We lurched forward.

"Yantes, Mother of Light, may your radiance burn eternal—"

"C'mon," I said, nudging him toward the stern.

The crew's eyes slid past us, skirting our hobbling form as they would the midday sun—or a cawing trio of ravens at the port's mouth. *Never look a curse in the eye.*

We shuffled aft. Overhead, tattered sails whisked and snapped.

A new shape formed in the mist, squat and hunched. Silence, standing at the foot of the stairs to the poop deck. He stepped forward and reached for Aldred's gun. Aldred let go of me to stop Silence's hand, swaying on his wounded leg. The mechanic paused and stared at him, unapologetic, unharried.

"Mentanillo," Aldred said.

Silence considered the wounded man.

"You owe me, Silas."

The mechanic shrugged, nodded up toward the wheel, shrugged again.

Silence reached out and pulled Aldred's gun free. Aldred didn't move. The Mech Lead shook the cartridges out into his hand. They looked like a pile of tiny harvester fuses in his broad palm. He disappeared them into his coat pockets. Lightning flashed. One bullet slid back into a chamber.

Then he handed the gun to me. The weight of it surprised me, bending my wrist. I firmed up around it.

The mechanic stumped off, and Aldred watched him go. I offered the gun to Aldred. He took it, leaning heavily on me as he used both hands to check the last cartridge. He snapped the gun shut.

"You don't carry, do you?" he asked.

"Not yet," I said.

He put the gun in my hand. I took the hefty thing and held it awkwardly.

"Now you do," he responded. "Don't let her push you."

He limped toward the stairs, toward the wheel. I snaked the gun into my coat, between the buttons. It settled into my inner chest pocket, the handle protruding enough to grab. The lumpy coat hid it well. In a few quick steps, I got back under Aldred's arm and helped him up the last steps to the poop deck.

Lightning flashed to show us the shadow of the Captain in the mist. Straight-backed, stick-limbed, standing a skeleton's vigil at the wheel.

"Strip down, Harken, and put this on!" the Captain shouted the moment we made the landing.

She threw me a bundle of cloth. The wind nipped at its edges when it flew my way. I caught it with my free hand.

The shimmering fabric oozed through my fingers. Soft and black, but with hard, thin rods running through it. Rods as light and pliable as bird bones. I let it unfold before me. Rods splayed out to form a wing, spanning down the side of a human shape, like the shadow of some black-winged demon. It looked my size. Wet winds licked the fabric and made it dance. Lighting crackled and made it rise in my hands. Eager.

"It'll kill her!" Aldred shouted. It startled me.

"Maybe."

Aldred looked at me, glancing down at my chest, at the awkward lump there. I reached a hand into my coat and found the cold handle.

"Kill me," the Captain blurted. "And you'll never know."

In slow and measured movements, I gripped the gun, pulled it from my coat, and pointed it at the Captain. She grinned ahead into the storm. My thumb went up to the hammer and rested there, swinging in the chaos as *Sheila* touched the heart of Kartheros.

Frustrated gales raked the gunwales and shoved at our bodies. The mists ran rampant. They trembled in the fiber of *Sheila's* decking. As she rolled, the Captain roved in my sights.

"It'll work, girl!" she shouted. "You want it to work!"

Lighting sparked, then and rumbled in our chests. Impossibly close. Kartheros called. Beckoned. My heart trembled.

I handed Aldred the gun.

He took it without meeting my eyes, then stepped back to lean against the railing. He stared down at the deck as mist whipped through his beard.

I removed my boots; the slimy deck boards seemed to writhe beneath my bare feet. I uncinched my waist belt to give myself room to change within my coat, pulling my arms in and working the rest of my clothes into a pile at my feet.

"Not a stitch of cloth on you," the Captain shouted. "Just the suit."

Lightning flashed above and below. The Captain smiled.

Hands trembling, I winced at the cool touch of the metallic fabric. The suit had a small opening at the neck, which I found easy to pry open. Fabric, but rubbery, elastic yet firm, and spun through with strands of metal. The rivets plucked painfully at my leg hairs as they slid down, fabric snugged in tight to every inch of my frame. I shimmied it over my waist. Slipped in one arm, then the other. My fingers slid into the gloved hands perfectly. Everything fit perfectly, from my narrow feet to my broad shoulders. She'd never once measured me. I cursed her name under my breath.

I felt the suit winding itself back together across my shoulders; an unseen spring bound it to me.

Bending my arms, I found that I had just enough slack to reach the top button of my coat. The oilskin slaked off, puddling around my feet.

Immediately, mist beaded up on my shimmering body and rolled away in the wind. I lifted my arms and examined the fabric wings. They gave a mellifluous metallic swish when I waved them.

I couldn't feel the wind. Even my coat had let more breeze through than this. The suit hugged and outlined my form at every curve, the material stretching and contracting to fit every inch of me.

Between my legs, a silvery wing spanned. I spread my arms, and two metal-boned wings opened, connecting down my side to my knees. A tiny metal snick came from my shoulders as thin rails unfolded from my front and back. Smaller versions of *Sheila's* lightrails.

Motion drew my eye up. Another fist of cloud emerged from the port side storm cell, billowing toward us. Fury.

The Captain spun the wheel, but too late. It smashed us broadside and rolled *Sheila* far to starboard. Wind ripped around us, spinning the crew's screams up past the bridge. Aldred's grip slipped off the railing. He stumbled across the poop deck, down toward the starboard gunwale. I leaped toward him, hoping to catch a line—or that the Captain could right the *Sheila* before we went over.

I touched Aldred's fingers and climbed his hand up to snatch his coat sleeve, close enough to see the terror through his goggles.

Lightning whited out everything. The suit jerked me back, flinging me up toward the wheel, trying to rip me from Aldred. I curled my fingers in, even as my shoulders screeched at his weight. The lightning pulled me back, and I dragged Aldred with me. *Sheila* righted, and we collapsed together at the feet of the Bent Nail. She stood at the wheel, bow-legged and laughing.

Hot, wet breath puffed on my neck. Aldred babbled, incoherent, into my ear. I wormed my way out from under him, then grabbed his arm and pulled him around. He helped a little, sitting back against the poop deck railing. He let his legs splay before him, hands face up in his lap. Glass pebbles of water dotted his bristles and lenses. His lips ran in circles. Suddenly, I recognized the prayer, remembered every word.

Yantes, Mother of Light,

may your radiance burn eternal.

Tear our eyes from the darkness.

Guide us through shadow with your grace,

through fear with your love.

Yantes, Mother of Light...

I stepped back, shaking. Droplets of water flicked off my limbs—my wings.

A deep rumble of thunder washed over us.

Power.

Thrumming, pulsing, unadulterated power. The heartbeat of a god.

The heart of Kartheros drummed against my own. Vast. Foreboding. Taunting me, tempting me.

"Go on, girl! *Sheila* will find you!"

His winds whipped at my braid, tugging it toward the stern. On numb legs, I tottered toward the ship's aft railing. I swung my legs around, awkward and clumsy, then hesitated on the slippery wood, clutching it tight as I balanced there.

The bottomless mist of Kartheros swirled beneath me. Faros waited below.

The Captain laughed. The wind howled. Sails whined. *Sheila* moaned.

We heard a sharp crack from up toward the bow and a piteous scream. More shouts rose. A flicker of orange danced into the mist, flashing to either side of the ship.

Captain Layla Nefferson cursed to wake the dead. I heard the wheel spin furiously. *Sheila* canted hard to port.

"Jump, damn you! Fly!"

My grip strained, slipped. Lightning flashed high above, and my rails tugged on my back. Kartheros' heart beat against my own.

I let go.

In the end—that very last moment—I leapt out into the storm.

The sudden free fall shot cold terror through my veins. I screamed.

An image flooded my mind, the gulls at port, wings spread, tensed, gliding on the winds. I snapped my arms out and the wings filled like tiny sails with a brutal *whump*. The force of it ground my shoulders back in their sockets, straining the fabric.

Another lightning ring flashed.

My neck hooked down as the lightning dragged me skyward, crushing my throat and choking me, pinning my arms to my side. I gurgled for air but couldn't force my throat open.

My ascent slowed. Slowed further. I snapped my head up to suck in a breath, coughing and crying into my goggles. Then—the top of the lift—a weightless breath. My sodden braid lifted from my back; my blood felt loose in my veins.

My momentum shifted. Still gasping, I began to fall again. I flexed my chest and shoulders.

My wings riffled, then filled with wind. Metal creaked along my back. I opened my wings and felt a sharp jab in my shoulder blade. I ignored it, focusing on controlling my fall.

The storm cells grumbled to one another. I braced my neck.

flash

Streaking blue light just above my head. I flexed back, keeping my spine taut from my neck to my heels.

I soared. Up. Up. Mists nipping at my face.

The mists grew choking, and I sipped air through my nostrils, trying to sneak breaths between the thickest bands of cloud. The strain grew, my back ached, then started to cramp.

flash

My vision went white. I thought I'd gone blind. I thought I'd died.

The bolt seared past, heat hissing through the mist.

My climb slowed. My eyes adjusted.

With the tiniest puff of air, I broke through the wall of a storm cell, and sudden sunlight pierced my goggles. I cursed and squinted.

Mountains of moisture bloomed, rose, contracted. Burning sunlight bounced from peak to peak, jettisoning rainbows from cloud to cloud and casting everything in a perfect golden hue. I can hardly describe how it struck me. The caps and peaks of Kartheros. Woolen towers, their crystalline heights glinting as they sailed past one another. Forming and unforming. And endless dance.

Light. Everywhere, light. The suit grew warm on my skin. The caps mumbled to one another, tiny bolts of lightning zipping to and fro between them. The storm stretched on and on, its cells interweaving out to every horizon.

I could fly forever like this, untouchable. Free. A queen of the sky.

I laughed aloud and wiggled in glee, reveling.

Yantes, Mother of Light...

Marking the direction of the sun, I started a gentle turn, swooping around the nearest billowing white protrusion. The column blossomed, small mounds of vapor emerging as I swept around it.

Gentle winds drew me down, but consistent arcs of lighting from the bulbous tower held me up.

A quiet balance.

I almost cried at the peace of it.

I felt a sudden, slight tug on my back. Firm pulses. A bulb of pressure pulled across the skin and down into my flesh. It pulsed, grew, then faded.

Another shot of cold fear slipped into my veins. I raced through a host of worries, wondering if the suit had started to come apart or if the pulse was some power storage cell that could spark and short out my spinal column.

Spiraling.

The fields of cloud suddenly looked insubstantial. A hundred leagues of open water separated Kartheros from the islands. I couldn't fly home.

A surge of frustration and rage.

I needed the *Sheila*.

I needed the Bent Nail.

I had to go back.

I felt another tug in my lower back—pulsed and rhythmic—not a malfunction. It tugged down and subtly to my left. As I turned around the cloud, the direction of the nudges shifted, pulling toward my tailbone.

A lodestone. To the Sheila.

Silly to think she'd let her precious experiment fly off without a way to retrieve it.

I savored the grace and light of my crystalline kingdom, taking a final gliding turn around the billowing column.

The pull came again—toward Faros below, but now pointing straight up my spine.

I pictured the swooping terns working by the seaports. Wings tucked, diving. I pinned my arms close and clenched my legs together.

The sudden drop stuttered my heart, and I popped my wings open again with a small cry.

I pictured the terns again, the crook in their wings, half-bent. I set my wings again, halfway out with bent elbows, and dove down into the boiling mass of clouds, punching through their false ceiling with less than a whisper.

Mist engulfed me and raced past. The speed pinned my cheeks back to my skull, and the frazzled ends of my hair tickled my neck in the wind. Lashing winds nipped and nudged me. Lightning cracked and flashed, but it barely slowed my dive.

I streaked through the madness of the storm, riding the edge of raw power and fragile mortality. A smile crept back across my face.

The tug at my back came again.

Up. Aft.

I'd missed her. She passed above me. Faros waited below. I fought back the panic, scanning the mists below me for a glimpse of the evil sea.

Yantes, Mother of Light—

I braced my back and spread my wings.

flash

The strain lifted me, swift and sure.

Distant lightning brought a blue glow to the clouds around me. I turned hard, carving a wide circle as I soared up, searching the squirming mists for any sign of a vessel.

Straight lines formed in the miasma; a sharp shadow emerging from the gloom. I turned toward it.

Sheila swept into view; holes in her sails, foremast crooked. Too fast. She grew rapidly. Dark shapes clumped along the bow. The crew, searching the mists. Lightning cracked and threw me skyward toward her. Wind stung my cheeks and peeled them back.

I would crush myself against her bow or miss her entirely and fly into the storm again. We'd swing back and forth like that forever, never falling, never touching.

Fear clutched at me again. Now that I'd seen her, I wanted to land. Wanted to feel her deck beneath my feet.

She tacked to starboard. I felt a surge of hope and relief.

I can veer to port. Match her turn.

I twisted my wings, turning hard.

We'll meet halfway, graceful, and I'll land—

My right wing wobbled, then snapped.

My wings crumpled and I catapulted up. I missed the bow by a few feet, goggled faces staring agape, hands darted out to grab at me, but missed. Tumbling and shrieking, I clipped the skyward lightning net and hurtled into the mists.

A shout from the crow's nest faded behind me.

I arced high, tumbling, slowing. Weightless seconds. My heart pounded, and my brain felt too large for my skull. I snapped out my wings, trying to gain some control. My left wing held firm, but the right flapped uselessly. Cursing, I spread my legs wide and tried to balance my awkward flight.

Kartheros bit me with cold winds, but I focused on stabilizing my fall. I leveled out. I lived. I flew. On the edge. Just on the edge.

The mists thinned, then flickered, then disappeared.

Faros.

The sight drained me of all hope and joy. Mountains of water swept across the surface, tall as the clouds above. Their peaks frothed and crashed, lashed by the winds of Kartheros. Faros would swallow me whole without malice or joy. Without notice.

I screamed as I fell.

The pulse at my back came: *hard to port.*

Sheila.

She lumbered down out of the clouds, matching my fall. Clear of the mists, she looked like a clunky freight wagon thrown from the heavens by a discontented godling. The waves dwarfed her as she fell toward them. She looked lost. *Where are her lower lightrails?*

Stowed away. They planned to land. On the wild face of Faros, beneath the heart of Kartheros. The audacity. The hubris. The Bent Nail.

A gargantuan peak of water swept beneath me, dragging a gust of wet wind. It snapped at my wings and slathered me with salt spray. I winced, but it passed and I dropped into the trough beyond it.

A perfect stillness came to me in that damp valley. The wind died. The slate gray back of the receding wave slipped away as the distant face approached.

A tiny lip on the back of the wave rose up and clipped my foot.

My limbs bent in a thousand unpleasant directions; arms ripping akimbo, knees bashing each other, then my own mouth, neck arcing back, then snapping down. Water crushed my goggles into my eyes, then ripped them away. It shunted into my nose, mouth, even my ears. My eyelids billowed and my mouth filled with salty water.

It ended.

Consciousness flickered. I lay tangled in the wings, face up, immobilized. Pain sprang up from my twisted shoulders. My lungs hacked, and viscous fluids bubbled up, foaming in my mouth. I spat them away, gasping for air.

Icy tendrils of salt water wormed their way into the suit, chilling me. They trickled into my throbbing ears and crept toward my swollen lips. Eager but not rushed, Faros savored these tender moments before he dragged me just another inch below into his unyielding depths.

A gray blanket of clouds swirled above.

High above, it crinkled and crumbled as if it tickled Kartheros' tender belly.

The motion changed beneath me, and I began to rise up the wave's face. This little tug of water as I rose, the gentle shift, just enough to pull the surface over my lips. I strained my neck but couldn't lift far enough to breathe. I snorted water out of my nose, nostrils flaring as I sucked in a last breath.

The wave above broke in earnest, tumbling down toward me. The roar came muted and distant to my submerged ears.

A frigid screen of water closed over my face. I shut my eyes.

Darkness. The final darkness. It deepened, a shadow passed above me. I cringed, waiting for the crash, for Faros to take me below.

thud

Something slammed into my chest and drove me further under, blasting my final breath away in a burst of bubbles. I went down, down into darkness, with fire in my lungs.

A cumbersome shape encircled me, clutching me tight. Arms. Arms wrapped around me. My eyes opened, but a rheumy wash of bubbles clouded everything.

The burn in my lungs grew. They screamed for air, screamed for help. Panic gripped me then, and I fought. I thrashed about, lashing against the suit, against what had wrapped around me, against anything, everything between my lungs and sweet air.

A sudden, brutal tug came; the thing that had fallen on me pulled back, dragging me with it. A rush and roar of fury swept in, the bellows of Faros crashing all around and the rumble of Kartheros above.

I hauled in a massive breath, shaking my head to clear my eyes. My skull smashed into something spongy but firm, and I heard a grunt. Silence, wrapped around me like a massive starfish feeding on an abandoned corpse. A chain around his waist trailed up to the dripping wet hull over our heads. The keel of *Sheila*—still airborne. Salvation.

I glimpsed the wave just a moment before it crashed into us.

Chaos. The wave drove us together, then tried to rip us apart. Silas latched tighter, and we tumbled down, a directionless, whirling mass of grays and blues all around. Cold metal hit my face, then dragged across it and away. *Slack chain. Sheila?* We tumbled into Faros. I caught glimpses down into the endless black depths, then the light above. In just those few seconds, my lungs burned for air again.

Darkness. Light. The abyss. The heavens. A massive, dark shadow lurched past on the surface.

My vision flickered and went dark. The panicked stutter of my heart crescendoed, then faded, curiously, into a serenity. My lungs went numb. Silence, but for the muted shushing of the whitewater above. Stillness within reach.

I ebbed away from the pain, grateful, eager even. Faros embraced me.

A deeper peace than I'd ever known...

I came back in a blue flash. Pain lanced through every thread of muscle and sinew in my body. My back bent deeply enough to stretch my lungs taut.

I slammed down on a hard surface, bouncing on my shoulder, then resting face down. Water gushed out of my chest, sloughing out of my nose and mouth. I heaved in a shallow breath.

Wood. Wet. Slick. Smooth.

Fibers swollen with perpetual damp.

Ship deck. Sheila.

I coughed and spat up bloody phlegm. A weight pressed on my head, forcing my mouth and nose into the deck boards. Breaths came small and hard. The burn. My lungs ached.

A sudden roar of sound swept me up with it. Shouting and cursing, stomping and crashing. Thunder. Thunder rolling in.

The weight lifted from my back. I heaved in a breath, and it was everything—all I could think about was the sweetness of that breath.

Shouts and cries. Close by.

Stand back!

—bodies—

Dead!

Dead?!

MOVE.

The Bent Nail. Above me. Her face twisted, filling all my flickering vision. Spiteful. Curious. Apathetic. A hand darted out. My broken wing twisted back and forth. Dull pain shot through my shoulder. She disappeared, shouting. The orders drifted back to me, tossed and clipped by the winds.

Get that suit—

> *—carry — below—*

> > *—toss overboard.*

Hands swept in all together, lifting me up.

My head lolled and I hung suspended. Upside down, Silence sprawled on the deck, still. Too still. Face gaunt and thin without his goggles, eyes stretched open.

He stared up—into the lightning of Kartheros.

I turned my head to follow his gaze.

flash

A beautiful, perfect ripple of blue light slid past above us. It scorched my bare eyes.

I cried out, pain mingling with rapture.

They dragged me below deck, my heels bumping the stairs. They dropped me in the hold, peeling the suit off and taking it away.

I heard Aldred nearby, still praying to Yantes.

The dark swallowed us. My open eyes saw only the brilliant yellow echoes of a lightning ring.

I wept as they faded.

The Art Of Procrastination

a procrastinated piece, prepared while procrastinating.

Procrastination is often considered a vice, an obstacle to productivity, and a bad habit to break. It is the act of delaying tasks or responsibilities despite knowing that the delay may cause negative consequences. Many view procrastination as an unproductive behavior, a personal flaw to be overcome in order to succeed. However, when examined more closely, procrastination emerges as something more complex than simply putting off work. It can be seen as an art form—a subtle, psychological dance between pleasure, guilt, indulgence, and avoidance, which can leave one feeling paradoxically both relieved and regretful.

The idea that procrastination is an art, however, requires a shift in perspective. It is not just an obstacle but a choice. Procrastinators are often highly skilled in the art of distraction, creative in finding new ways to delay tasks, and expert in rationalizing their inaction. This behavior is frequently associated with a sense of comfort in the moment—an escape from immediate discomfort. Yet, it is precisely this temporary relief that can later lead to greater stress and regret. As the famous quote states: "Procrastination is like masturbation, it feels good at first, but then you realize you just screwed yourself."

At its core, procrastination is a form of instant gratification. People procrastinate because they seek short-term pleasure or relief. The looming pressure of a deadline, the tedium of an unappealing task, or the fear of failure can prompt an individual to avoid facing the task at hand. Instead, they opt for activities that offer immediate rewards—scrolling through social media, watching a TV show, checking email, or even doing low-stakes work that feels productive but isn't truly important. These distractions can bring temporary satisfaction, but they also accumulate into a sense of guilt and anxiety when the deadline draws near. It's the classic pattern: procrastination offers a fleeting sense of pleasure or relief, but at the cost of long-term consequences.

The irony of procrastination is that it often makes the task at hand feel more daunting the longer it is delayed. In the beginning, the task may seem manageable, but with time, the pressure builds and the task grows more intimidating. The fear of failure, the fear of not meeting expectations, and the growing weight of the unfinished task can spiral into anxiety. But rather than tackling the task, the procrastinator may continue to indulge in distractions and diversions supplying the instant gratification to avoid the anxiety of potential failure. This pattern reinforces the cycle of procrastination, creating a feedback loop of anxiety to avoidance to gratification to guilt to anxiety. The loop continues all while hoping for a sudden burst of inspiration to break the pattern.

However, not all procrastination is inherently negative. In some cases, putting off a task can lead to improved performance. Some people thrive under the pressure of a looming deadline, finding that they work best when they are forced to focus under time constraints. In these instances, procrastination may be an adaptive strategy. The key, however, is balance. If procrastination becomes chronic, if it prevents the individual from ever completing tasks or leads to negative consequences, it becomes a serious problem.

Ultimately, procrastination is a complex phenomenon that involves more than simple avoidance. It is a form of psychological negotiation, where the procrastinator weighs the short-term pleasure of avoidance against the long-term costs of inaction. The act of procrastination is an art—a blend of self-deception, avoidance, and sometimes even productivity in disguise. But the lesson that procrastination teaches is simple: while it may feel good in the moment, the long-term consequences of procrastination are rarely satisfying. The immediate pleasure of avoiding responsibility, like the fleeting thrill of self-indulgence, eventually gives

way to regret and the realization that more work is needed. Just as the quote reminds us, "you just screwed yourself."

Prompted by a patron, ChatGPT penned this essay and Bing AI created the art.

The Bluff,
As Explained to My Cat

He scratched his temple with the laser pistol and shifted the weight of his backpack. It looked heavy. I didn't know his name. I had taken to calling him Slouch in my head. He slouched from the ground up. He'd clearly been a sloucher his whole life. One slouch away from melting into the ground. And he was doughy. And when the wind switched, I could smell him. Musty.

All more or less how my Uncle Chester had described him. We worried he might try something like this, Uncle Chester and I.

I watched a tiny drop of sweat trickle around his eyebrow. One slid down my own face, too. June sun beat down on the hilltops of western Massachusetts. The heat had started draining the green from the grasses, and I didn't love it. My skin was burning. I shaded my face with one hand, slowly, with an eye on his gun. Musty. Slouchy. Jumpy.

Just behind me, the fusion drive of my brand new two-man flier hummed, rising and falling as it idled. The rhythm comforted me.

"So, like—" the man with the laser pistol mused, "what's to stop me from just killing you, taking those goodies, and keeping my money?" The weight and heft of his Boston accent made my head spin a little.

My arm grew tired, so I lowered it. Slowly.

I blink a lot. Especially when I'm stressed. And Slouch, waving his gun and getting greedy, made me nervous. Interestingly, my blinking sometimes makes other people nervous. Typical negative feedback cycle.

I stared straight into Slouch's eyes and blinked a few times. He stared back and tried not to.

I knew that a round from that gun would melt through my flesh and bones in nanoseconds and have heat left over to bore a steaming ten-foot hole into the hill behind me.

My breath tightened a little bit, and the blinking got worse. His pistol shook.

• • •

I'd bought the flier with cash.

I sold my studio apartment in Harlem "as is"; meaning it reeked of weed and cat piss, then went to the bank.

The cash from the apartment sale fit neatly into my backpack, though the weight had surprised me. The teller had given me one of the looks I get sometimes. The one when I'm doing a crazy thing. No one carries cash because no business accepts cash. Yet there I stood, withdrawing millions and millions of actual, physical, anachronistic dollars. And blinking too much. And not making eye contact. Anachronistic. I like that word. And anachronism. It's an old favorite. Hard and soft in all the right places. Tough to say, but I loved the sound it made when it worked. I said it under my breath once or twice, let the feel of it roll around on my teeth.

"Mawrp?" my cat called from her carrier. "Mawrp?"

She wasn't used to the carrier. She wanted the apartment back. I kind of did, too. No. I really did. I wanted my life back. But. No one wanted us there, in New York. Well. She would have been fine, probably. Stray cats can do well in the city. Better than a lot of people, I guess. Cats know how to be alone in a crowd. I thought I did, too. The crowd had started giving me more and more funny looks lately. Natural-borns are rare these days. Natural born and neurodivergent? Not many of us at all. Maybe just me.

So I just had Mindy. And she had me.

"You must really like Trump's face, huh?" the teller said. "You a collector or something?"

I did not like Trump's face. Nor did I like this pudgy, sweaty, youthful teller with their wafer-thin mustache and their too-thin tie and their squirminess. Their name tag read: Ainsley. I didn't like it. It felt like an ugly word.

I counted down from five in my head—to delay my response. Best not to speak right away. People don't always like the first thing I think to say. I followed the teller's terrified glances down to the counter. A little green Trump grinned up at us from the top of the stack of crisp $1,000 bills.

"Oh," I said, "Yeah. I— c-collect. Ana—Anachronisms."

I took a breath and let the tension out of my gut and back. I don't mind speaking, but other people seem to mind when I do. The teller stared at me for another moment. I pictured, for a split second, what

Ainsley would look like on the front line of a rally. Frothing at the mouth. Chanting about how I shouldn't be allowed to reproduce. Or work near their kids. Or their parents. Or even breathe the same air. I imagine Ainsley wished they could call and report me to someone. But. I wasn't doing anything illegal. Just weird.

• • •

The dealer had mentioned a price for the two-man flier before launching into a breathless gush of how it would change my life. I'd tried to accept the initial offer and pay with the cash, but his mouth never closed. I could see his molars when he declared this model the "ultimate bachelor's coupe." His grin made my skin itchy.

Just between us boys, we both know how many fine, fine-looking lovers you'll woo in this bad Jackson. Heh heh. Am I right, son? Carving up the air, landing at the helipad of the party, stepping out with that fine, fine passenger on your arm. Letting the autopilot hang it on the building for you while you take a sip of the refreshments. Mmm-mm. Then, later, the autopilot flies you home while you find more (darting eyes and scandalous pause) interesting things to do in the passenger seat. Or the spacious cargo bay.

A cool cup of water sat in front of me. I sipped it for something to do other than listen to him yammer about the sex appeal of the flier. I knew I didn't have a lot of sex appeal, but I also knew that if I wanted it, I probably couldn't buy it. His whole story rested on the premise of landing at a party. Unlikely. The cargo space was adequate.

"So, on top of the killer *look* of the thing," the dealer said slowly, grasping for a new tack, "the autopilot is tippy-top notch. Best in class. Guaranteed smooth flight, in and out of the busiest skies. Perfect synchronicity with all other air traffic. No sweat."

It was odd, letting him talk himself out. He kept pitching the thing I'd already decided to buy, and I didn't know how to stop him.

"Mawrp?" Mindy asked.

He glanced down at her carrying crate and opened his mouth to ask the question. When his eyes got back to mine—he shut his mouth. I did too good a job of making eye contact, I think. He was looking away more than I was, and that's usually a bad sign.

Fine. I took that opportunity to name my price. I opened the back-pack, and he leaned back in his chair with wide eyes as if I had cotton-mouth snakes in the bag. Cottonmouths kill quickly, but they're easy to spot.

But I didn't have cottonmouths. I had a backpack full of anachro-nisms. And some clothes. Stuffed down at the bottom. Having the cash on top made more sense.

"So, d— d-d— do we have a d-d-deal?" I asked, like you're supposed to and looked him directly in the eye, like you're supposed to. Then I blinked hard, twice, and ruined it. *Shit.* My abs ached and I felt the slight flush in my face.

"Uhm... I just need to check a few things," he said, standing abruptly, "with my manager."

"That's fine," I said, leaning back as if I were comfortable in the chair. "I c-c-cleared my d-d—"

"Day?" he filled in.

"Schedule. I — c-c-cleared my schedule for this."

Hazy morning sunlight flicked across his face, glinting on his glasses. Probably fake. Real glasses cost more than eye surgery. Anachronisms were hip. Some were, anyway. He left to chat with his manager. I let out a breath.

"Mawrp," Mindy lamented from the crate. I sympathized.

I looked around the office. Spartan. Minimalist. Digital. All lit-up displays and glistening faux metal. Except for the fake plants. A row of them by the window, on a bed of fake dirt. I took Mindy out of her cage and placed her on the plants. She defecated and peed. I waited for her to finish, then helped her back into her crate.

The dealer returned. He paused in the doorway, sniffing the air, puzzled and perturbed. I don't think he saw the little pile of cat scat in the plants, but I caught him shooting a suspicious glare at the crate as he sat down.

Less than an hour later, I flew out of the dealership in a shiny new flier with Mindy and a mostly empty backpack. I didn't feel any sexier than I had, but a new sense of freedom floated around the cabin with me. I had left the passenger seat in the parking lot. They'd called to tell me about it. I told them to keep it and to please never call me again. Then I hung up and flew myself to Uncle Chester's.

• • •

Flying is nice because it's quiet. In blissful silence, I made modifications to the personal aircraft. The manuals all read very clearly that you shouldn't tinker with it in mid-air. Logical but inefficient. Besides, I'm good with software and wiring. I quickly disabled the government trackers and a few other flight speed and maneuverability restrictions that I didn't think we'd need. I worked in the back of the flier for a while, preparing my backup plan. The engine purred and purred. Fusion. Limitless power. The miracle of flight, accessible to the wealthy masses, but new to market. Still a little pricey, but not more than a studio apartment in Harlem.

When I was done, I put on power ballads from way back. I like power ballads. The largeness of the guitar, the heart of the vocals, the persistent percussion. Mindy likes power ballads now, too. She hadn't at first, but I started playing them softly while we slept in the apartment, and they grew on her. We like things that make us feel safe, and the things we listen to while we're safe make us feel safe. She explored the cabin for a while at first, with a handful of *mawrps* to let me know she had her doubts about it. I finished making my adjustments to the ship and nestled back into the pilot's chair. It reclined into a comfortable bed; that much, at least, the sweaty man at the dealership had not oversold. Sunlight bounced through the broad windshield on my lap and chest. Mindy curled up with some pawing and purring. We napped in the sun for the rest of the flight.

• • •

A soft chime from the autopilot woke me. The green blanket of pine canopy rose up, and my flier slid under it into a large clearing. We landed softly on the grassy lawn between my Uncle Chester's commercial greenhouse and rustic cottage.

I exited through the cargo bay, Mindy's crate in hand. Chester greeted us, beaming, like he always does. I like Uncle Chester. His real name is Charles, but he thinks Chester is more fun to say. I kind of get that.

"Great to see you!" he shouted as the low whine of the turbines trailed off to a gentler hum.

He wrapped me up in a hug that I returned with one arm. He smelled of pot and pine trees. He loved gardening and taking long walks in the woods.

"I take it the apartment sale went through?" he asked, releasing me and stepping back to gawk at my new aircraft. He wore jeans and a flannel shirt, as always, and the jeans were pulled over the tops of his big boots, as always. And, as always, his face reminded me of my dad's.

Logical. Expected.

Still.

Old grief clutched at my heart and loss soured my face. Chester's smile faltered. I caught my expression and tried to turn it around. *Chester,* I thought. *This is Uncle Chester. Dad's gone. Like he wanted. Let him go. Show Chester you love him.* I attempted to smile, but I think I landed in a sort of benevolent grimace.

"Yeah, I sold my apartment," I said in a rush. "And then Mindy and I negotiated with real c-c-c- — money."

"Right..." he said, clasping his hands in front of him. "It's—we're glad to have you here, safe and sound."

He shook his clasped hands before him, staring at the ground. His hands slowed, then stilled. My synapses finally connected.

"Thank you," I said, "for taking me in. I tried—uhm—not to—"

"Of course," he said, eyes snapping up. Relieved, I think. His voice got a little low and a little shifty. "You're an independent guy. I get that."

"I—wanted to live alone. At first, I mean. But I'm glad to be here now."

"We're glad to have you," he said. It felt a little forced. He and Annette had never had children. They'd never wanted children. They'd treated me like an adult all my life. I liked it. Usually.

"Just for a bit," I said. "When I have enough to move out, you and Annette can have your space back. Or I'll get blown away by a drug dealer. Either way, I'll be gone. But you'll have to take care of Mindy. Or find her a new home."

"Mawrp," Mindy affirmed.

Damn. Chester looked upset. *Should have done a countdown.*

"We don't have to do this," he said. "We can call the whole thing off. There's other ways."

"No," I cut in. "This is fast and simple. Like we planned."

"Okay," he said. "At least let me go with you on the drop?"

"I removed the passenger seat," I said honestly. "To accommodate the cargo weight." Less honest.

"Of course," he said, eyes darting to the wide-open cargo bay, then back to me. He nodded. "Of course."

We paused there for a moment. I watched Chester think. His gaze wandered up through the pines as he roughed up the stubble on his chin. He shrugged to himself and looked back at me with a smile.

"Let's eat. Your Aunty Annie can't wait to see you."

Annette, Aunty Annie, was lukewarm about me at best. She didn't dislike me, but we really never had anything to talk about.

"Let's eat after," I said. "I don't want to be late."

"Alright, well, at least set your things down inside," he turned slightly toward the cabin. "I can show you your room?"

"I don't have much," I said, shrugging. "Just Mindy and a change of clothes, and they're flying with me."

"Okay, son," he said, "Okay."

I followed him to the greenhouse, and we loaded a pallet of cargo into the back of the flier.

• • •

Two new laws had passed in New York—Anti-Nature laws, as the liberals called them. The one that made it impossible for me to reproduce, which I felt indifferent about in practice, but incensed about in principle. Not that my feelings mattered much. The other created a business opportunity for the right people. Like Uncle Chester.

So I stood there with the back hatch of the flier open behind me, a pallet of dried mushrooms, marijuana, and LSD resting innocently in my tiny cargo bay. The hills of Massachusetts rolled away all around us. Summer sun beat down.

And Slouch stood before me, having second thoughts. Greedy thoughts. His fingers flexed on the grip of the laser pistol.

"Like, with this much to move, I can build my own empire in a month. I think maybe I don't need ya."

It scared me. A bit.

5...

4...

3...

Mindy gave us a long "mawrrrrp" from her carrier. She sounded suspicious and angry. Not mellow. Slouch jumped, making me flinch. I felt anger swelling up.

"Maybe you're not the r— right fit for us, either. Long t-t— term" I said. I let that linger for a second before moving on. "I'll d-d— discuss it with my uncle."

"Mawrp."

Greedy daydreams sliding from his face, Slouch stared at me. Then looked past into the cargo bay. Mindy's eyes glinted in the shadows. I pictured her pupils, thin slits, like a cottonmouth. Spooky. I liked it.

"You brought a fucking cat to a drug deal?" Slouch asked.

"Yes," I said. "And I can show you." Mindy hissed. I hadn't heard her do that before. "Not the cat. I don't think she likes you. I can show you a reason not to kill me."

I didn't like him either, but I managed not to say that out loud.

"What if something goes down, man? What would happen to the cat? Did you think of that?"

"No..."

"Well..." he started, then paused. "Well. Well, you should've. I'm not taking it in. I'll kill you and leave the dumb thing here. I'll do it."

I froze as my heart clenched. I hadn't considered that, which felt stupid and selfish, but I couldn't do anything about it now.

"Mawrp," Mindy interjected.

"Her," I said. "Her name is Mindy."

"Whatever, man!"

He screamed it in a high, angry voice, but his eyes didn't match it.

"Mawrp."

He squinted at Mindy, wrinkling his face. Sunlight popped and darted off the laser pistol as his hand shook. Sweat ran off his red, scrunchy face. But he didn't kill me, so I moved on.

"C-c- — can you see that cl-cl- — those numbers?" I asked, pointing up to the touch screen I'd hung so it faced the rear door. It was meant for the passenger's entertainment in-flight, but Mindy and I didn't need it. I had rewired it and put a big clock on it. It counted down; less than six minutes remained on it.

"So what? It's a clock. What about the stupid clock?"

"Do you see the wuh- wuh— —" Slouch glanced up at the wires, but let me finish— "the wires?" I asked. My abs burned and I felt sweat stick my shirt to my back.

"Yeah, bro, I see the fucking wires," he said. "You gonna make a fucking point before I burn a hole in you?"

"Hard for me to make a point after — so, yes." I didn't wait for him to catch up with me. "I d-d-destabilized the fusion reaction in th-th- this flier," I said in a slow and deliberate tone. "It will go cr-cr— It will m-m-"

Slouch stared at me, mouth ajar. I tried to relax. It didn't work.

"It will go cr-cr-cr— — critical," I sucked in a grateful breath, then rushed on, "in five minutes. In six minutes, this hill will t— — liquify. Massachusetts will evaporate."

He stared at me. My torso felt hollow despite the big breaths I drew in. I sagged in my drenched shirt.

"Evaporate" has a nice sound to it as well. None of the hardness of "anachronism," but a nice up-and-down rhythm to it.

Evaporate.

Cottonmouth venom is gelatinous and does not evaporate.

"Six minutes is also how fast a grown adult c-c-can die from a cottonmouth's poison. If the bite is in the right place," I said. "The wrong one, I mean. The throat."

Slouch had shut his mouth and then opened it again, so I stopped speaking. I counted down from five, breathing with each number. His finger toyed with the trigger as his face pinched.

"Are you fucking serious?" he asked.

"Yes," I replied, "Cottonmouth poison is highly effective."

"What?! No! You'd kill a whole state over a drug deal? And your own *cat?!*"

"Mawrp?"

"Oh! No," I said, giving him a confused look. "I wouldn't do that. Would you do that?"

"No!" Slouch spluttered. "But—"

"Oh good!" I interrupted him in my too-loud voice. "Then please leave your money in the c-c-c— bay." I stepped back so he could approach the flier.

Slouch paused. Considering. Scrunching. He scratched his head with the pistol.

Then he slank closer to me and the flier, suspicious and timid, yet slug-like. Slouch studied the clock, still scratching his temple with the pistol.

"Shit."

He snorted and shuffled his large backpack off, letting it clunk down on the open bay door. He slouched away from the flier.

I opened the backpack and calmly started to count the cash. Quickly, but one bill at a time.

Real, physical cash. As agreed. Another stack of anachronisms. More than I'd started with that morning.

"Fucking wild, using real money for this," he said. "Bank teller gave me this look—"

He cut short.

"Like you wuh—wuh— were crazy," I said, nodding. "I know. Please, d-d-don't talk, r–right now."

I kept counting. The timer ticked past the four-minute mark.

"You're not gonna... turn it off?" he asked, gesturing at the timer with his pistol.

"Obviously not. Not till wuh- — we leave the ground."

I concentrated on counting.

He stopped talking. Bills flowed through my fingers. Three minutes—two—

The timer hit the one minute before he interrupted again.

"Hey, man—"

"Finished," I blurted, grateful. It was all there. I could be rid of unseemly Slouch. Until next time. But that's business. You work with people you don't like. Usually. Except for Uncle Chester. I was lucky.

I stepped into the cargo bay. He looked up at me, deflated. The gun hung limp at his side.

"We'll call you when we need more," he said.

"Fine," I said and clicked the button to raise the door. The clock read thirty-five seconds. "Goodbye." Slouch stared at the timer as the door shut. I sat down in the pilot seat, fired up the engine, and took off. I let the autopilot take over. We circled the hill to get our heading for Chester's. I caught a last glimpse of Slouch, leaning on the pallet, staring up at us, shielding the sun from his eyes with the pistol, then we were away.

Unhurried, I peeled off my soaked outfit and changed into my spare clothes. I sat in the pilot's chair and reclined.

"Mawrp?" asked Mindy, hopping into my lap.

"It's c-called a bluff, Mindy," I said, stroking her fur and feeling my back muscles start to unwind. "The cl-clock isn't wired to anything."

"Mawrp?"

"Because people are scared," I said. "Bluff's work because people are scared."

0x4E 0x65 0x6F 0x6E
0x20 0x6C 0x69 0x67
0x68 0x74 0x73 0x20
0x73 0x68 0x69 0x6D
0x6D 0x6

0x44 0x72 0x69 0x66
0x74 0x69 0x6E 0x67
0x20 0x74 0x68 0x72
0x6F 0x75 0x67 0x68
0x20 0x54 0x6F 0x6B
0x79 0x6F 0x20 0x73
0x74 0x72 0x65 0x65
0x74 0x73 0x2C

0x46 0x61 0x6D 0x69
0x6C 0x79 0x20 0x77
0x65 0x20 0x73 0x65
0x65 0x6B 0x2E

neon lights shimmer
drifting through Tokyo streets
family we seek

Clan Traynham

Madison, Kristen, Charlotte, Cam

The Third Witch

The doorbell tinkled overhead and the colors of the dress shop exploded in Tabatha's eyes. A biting December gust hissed in on her heels, cutting through the folds of her long skirts. Muttered curses for the frigid winds came from Melanie behind her, drawing the twinge of a smirk to Tabatha's lips. The cold had never bothered her, but every year, the moment fall breezes soured into winter's frost, Melanie began to fuss.

Fragile rays of sunlight tumbled through the front window, streaking out across verdant emeralds, brazen scarlets, and the ripple of indigos. Cuts ranged from polite to downright scandalous. White lace sprouted from collars and crept like lichen from hem to hem. Halfway back, lurking in the shadows, a regiment of skeletal corsets stood in silent lines.

Tabatha moved her right hand to rest on her bulging belly as she waded into the wash of colors. Her eyes slid away from the corsets. It would feel strange to live without her bump. She could hardly remember where else she had rested her hands.

"Mrs. Moresly!" Elaine, the seamstress, slid through a curtain in the back wall with a seasoned smile. "Ready for your final round of maternity dresses?" She wore a muted pink frock with a narrow waist and a tall collar that ran right up to her chin. The smile faltered as Tabatha's sister clumped into the shop and kicked the door shut with a frustrated heel. "Oh and sister Melanie, as well! Both Edgecomb sisters in one morning, what a treat!"

Melanie bobbed a tiny mock curtsy at the shopkeeper and gave her the Devil's own grin. The ruby feather in Mel's hat wobbled precariously through the dip, as did her ample bosom. Neither of them corrected Elaine for the familiar use of their maiden name.

"No maternity dresses today, Miss Elaine," Tabatha said. "My sister requires—"

"Nothing!" Melanie cut in. "I have all I need in the blood of my veins and the *thrum-thrum-thrum* of my heart. Oh! This is nice..."

She stopped to lift the sleeve of the window display; a sage green gown, some delightfully talented seamstress had trimmed it with an ornate, fluid pattern, subtly floral. Elaine's narrow face cut through the gloom as she leaned forward.

"It would certainly flatter the lady's figure," Elaine ventured, "if I let it out a bit."

Melanie scowled and let the sleeve fall through her fingers.

"My figure needs no flattering," Melanie stated. "Apparently, it needs containing."

"I see. Did Mr. Whitten catch wind of the new corsets?" Elaine asked. She rested a hand on the protruding iron rump of a showcase. Melanie rolled her eyes, then slapped her own rear and pointed an accusatory finger at Elaine. She swept past Tabatha to better harangue the shopkeeper, jostling a rack of dresses as she went.

"Do you know—when I was twelve, just after Mother passed away, I realized that she'd given me these husband-winning-hips while my sister got those stunning eyes. I thought myself a clear victor."

Tabatha rolled her brilliant blue eyes. She could almost feel the specks of hazel in her irises drift around, her sister brought them up so often.

"But no! Despite having been wed and bed, my dear husband Charles still strongly suggests that I might adorn myself to his tastes! As if I must be fit for an iron saddle and bridle!"

Melanie clocked the frame of the corset with a knuckle. The display wobbled and tipped back. Elaine startled and caught the wiry frame with both hands.

"Oh, sorry," Melanie said, unabashed.

"No matter," Elaine muttered.

"Turning a fine mare in the peak of her health into a troubled ass, that's our work today!" Melanie continued. "Mother never stood for such nonsense!"

"Sister, please," Tabatha cut in with a soft touch on her Melanie's arm. Elaine had frozen with her shopkeeper's grin plastered to her face, both hands clutching the hips of the corset. "You're scaring Ms. Elaine. Let's just find a comfortable fit to accentuate your natural endowments and be on our way."

"Oh fine, be glib," Melanie huffed. "You can afford to, what with that little miracle growing in you and your husband finally leaving you in peace."

"It's not such a terrible fate," Tabatha said. "A family."

"Psh! I have everything I want, and more, in myself!" Melanie protested. "And fate seems to agree with me, despite all of Charles's fine attentions."

She shot a look back toward the green dress, the fingertips of one hand lingering on her stomach. Her brows knit together, reminding Tabatha sharply of their mother.

"Come now," Elaine said. She released the corset and reached out to cup Melanie's elbow. "Tell me your troubles and we will find a dress to address it in." The shopkeeper grinned at her own words, then gave the younger woman a gentle nudge. Melanie moved with her, deeper into the sea of fabrics, toward the rock-like corsets lurking in the shadowed depths. She scowled as she was led.

"And..." Elaine continued, "if we can't find quite the right fit for your worries, we'll perhaps discuss other, less conventional, recourse that you may wish to pursue..."

Elaine led Melanie over to one of the better polished ironworks and Tabatha let them go. Elaine would gossip and make airs about her dresses and hint at the procurement of tinctures, potions, or "prayers," which might help the afflicted. And, of course, she would wring Melanie dry for gossip. Melanie, for her part, would feign disinterest, monologuing on the injustices of womanhood.

Tabatha let her smile play on her lips and her baby gave an assertive kick. She knew that Melanie still held deep affections for her Charles, despite her disparagement of the great familial suicide of the female soul. Stuffing an ardent, full-bodied wife into a corset seemed ridiculous, granted, but even kind men could be ridiculous at times. Tabatha's own husband, Ernest, oscillated so quickly between warmth and cold distance that she struggled to maintain a hold of her own emotions. She worried that her mother found Tabatha's gilded position terribly impressive—but her babe would have a loving home, and the breadth of Ernest's estate ensured safety and contentment for her and even for Melanie, should something happen to Charles. Her dead mother's spite and disappointment could hardly provide all that.

Tabatha rubbed her stomach with a smile. It would be a girl. She knew it. As her mother had known when she'd had Tabatha. She knew it would have her mother's eyes, her own eyes.

Her child's spine would be her own, however. Though Auntie Melanie would no doubt help her firm it up.

"And what should your name be, little one?" Tabatha whispered down to her belly. She hummed for a few moments, letting the colors glide beneath her hands as she floated through the store. She felt soft movements.

"Virginia, perhaps?" The babe's sudden kick brought Tabatha a twinge of discomfort. "Not Virginia, very well. Perhaps a color? Violet?" Another small kick. "Marigold?"

The vicious jab nearly doubled her over. She grimaced at first, but grinned as she straightened. "Mmm—fine then. No colors and certainly no flowers."

A black dress hemmed in brilliant purples caught her eye. It had the sharpest lines of any in the store. It spoke of self-possession and severity; mischief. It drew a name to her lips.

"Morticia." Tabatha whispered down with a stroke of her belly. Nothing. Stillness. Then—a gentle, gliding touch. It had an almost pensive feel to it, if you could believe that kind of thing. The name rolled across Tabatha's tongue a few times, then nestled into the back of her mind. "Morticia. Yes. Welcome, Morticia, the world is ready."

A new pain erupted below the folds of her long skirt. One she had not felt before. One she expected, longed for, and dreaded. It terrified her.

"Oh," she said, trying to make it more than a mewl. "Melanie?"

The next contraction came.

"MELANIE!"

A crash of wire framing, a violent rustling of fabrics. Melanie appeared at her side, hiding her worry behind a bright smile.

Elaine rushed ahead to fetch the midwife.

· · ·

Tabatha nearly broke Melanie's hand during the birth. The pain was incredible. Unlike anything she'd ever experienced or expected.

Mothers and midwives talked about it, described it in detail, but they never did it justice. No one could. Drenched in her own sweat and blood, screaming, praying, cursing, Tabatha never once thought her sister might leave her side and she never did. Nor did she so much as wince at her sister's fierce grip. When Morticia did finally emerge, she arrived shrieking, but quieted quickly. Melanie helped the midwife clean and wrap the child. Tabatha caught the spark of longing in her sister's gaze. It disappeared in an instant and Melanie turned to her sister with the bundle, radiating joy.

"A girl!" Melanie shrieked. "And look! Look at her eyes! You're clairvoyant after all, Tabby!"

Tabatha smiled and took her bundled child.

"I will stay with you always," she whispered.

"We will," Melanie chirped, putting a hand on her sister's shoulder and gazing down at the child.

Tabatha smiled up at her, then promptly fell unconscious without loosening her grip.

• • •

Eleven Rather Uneventful Months Later

Morticia grew fast and strong. She rarely cried and attended the world around her with ceaseless observation. To Tabatha, it seemed the child had arrived in a world of mystery, with every intention of rooting out the meaning and mechanics behind everyday miracles.

It took months for Tabatha to recover from the birth. Just now, as winter crept in again, she felt strong again. A fire roared in the hearth, but Tabatha rocked in a chair by the window she'd cracked open. Morticia slept on her chest. A snowflake trembled down to land in the babe's dark hair. Tabatha took in air to blow it off, but hesitated.

She waited.

The snowflake melted and icy water dissipated into Morticia's wispy black hair. It trickled down to her skin. The child didn't wake, didn't even stir. Tabatha smiled, gave her a squeeze, and leaned down to kiss away the trickle of melted snow.

Tabatha heard the slam of the front door downstairs and the stomping of boots as Ernest shook off the snow. Careful of her sleeping child, Tabatha snaked a hand out and shut the window. Ernest appeared moments later.

"There's my darling wife," he said. "Bit of a chill in here? Did you have the window open again?"

"Of course not dear," Tabatha said softly. "Morticia might catch cold."

"Mmm, our boy won't mind half so much, I think," Ernest grumbled, ambling to the sideboard and pouring a tall glass of brownish liquor. He smelled of smoke and bourbon already. He wasn't an outright scoundrel, but certainly no stranger to the gentlemen's club of an afternoon. Tabatha could forgive him that.

"Well, she's tougher than we give her credit for, I think," Tabatha replied. "She'll make a fine heir to our line."

"A fine heir to *your* line, perhaps," Ernest said, not unkindly. He turned to her with a fresh glass and an expectant look, pleading. A tired question expecting a new answer. An icy feeling crept through Tabatha's veins. She forced out the same answer she'd been using for ten months.

"Soon, dear." She forced a smile, as well. "I'll be well enough for another soon."

Ernest gave her a rigid smile. Then his brows drew down, his chest swelled, and his mouth jerked open to form half a word. He paused.

The new father deflated and took a sip of his drink. He undid the buttons of his waist coat with care, before settling into the chair by the fire.

"Of course, dearest," he said. "When you're ready."

That age old pride. The preservation and continuation of the familial line. Maintaining good stock. In truth, she felt quite fine. Her body could bear another child. For reasons she couldn't point to or reason out, the thought of having a boy chilled her. And she knew, as she'd known before, that if she had another, it would be a boy. She'd not told Ernest that. She'd not even told Melanie.

The room felt stifling all of a sudden.

Tabatha rose in a rush and Ernest stood quickly to match her, surprised. They stared at one another for a moment. She could see him weigh the scales, frustration and faith, balancing. Tipping. He wouldn't wound her, not with words or hands, not if he could avoid it, but he needed a son. Pride demanded it.

Amelia, their Matron of the house, appeared in the doorway in her dark gray working skirts. She clucked and cast a stern glance toward the window.

"Quite a chill in here," she said. "Is Ms. Morticia ready for her bed?"

"Yes..." Tabatha said, looking away from Ernest. "These windows get drafty when the wind switches. We're both ready for bed, I believe."

Ernest's eyes followed her out; hurt and longing floated on the surface of his nascent belligerence. Yes, time for her to be abed, indeed.

• • •

Tabatha awoke with a start. A storm raged without. Winter winds howled as they whipped past the large house. Shutters clacked and banged all along the stone walls. Something felt... wrong. Not just the storm. Tabatha felt a directionless sense of dread. It knotted her stomach around her spine. Sweat popped on her brow.

The new mother rose in silence and found her slippers in the dark before padding to her door. She opened it quietly, despite the rage of the storm, then tiptoed past Ernest's door to reach the nursery. She stumbled in her groggy half-sleep, but prised the nursery door open with care. The wind whistled in a crook of the exterior walls and grew louder as the door opened, then softened as she shut it behind her. Morticia's bassinet stood in the far corner, away from the bitter cold of the windows. Tabatha put a hand on the rocking chair beside the bassinet. A gust of wind slammed a shutter, startling Tabatha, but the babe didn't stir. The mother watched her child's tiny chest rise and fall. She smiled and resisted the urge to snuggle her. *Safe*. She was safe.

Tabatha turned to the windows, watching the snowflakes beat themselves against the panes, listening. The whistling wind came again and Tabatha heard now that it sounded louder and closer than it should.

A tiny drift of snow on the window sill. A window had been cracked open, just an inch.

Frowning, Tabatha crossed the room and shut it. She glared out at the swirling torrents of snow and ice, watching the shadows curdle. Nothing sinister. Nothing of note. Nothing at all, aside from snow and shadow. Brow still furrowed, Tabatha went to the rocker by the bassinet and sat down. Morticia slept on, heedless to the storm and her mother's worry.

As the storm wore itself down, Tabatha drifted to sleep by her babe.

• • •

The door's creak woke Tabatha. As she blinked her eyes open, Ernest poked his head and shoulders into the nursery. Crisp light bounced through the windows of the nursery. Her husband gave her a kind grin, almost apologetic. She noticed the forest green of his favorite cloak already on his shoulders.

"Good morning, dearest," he said. She blinked at him.

"I'm off to meet the Sheriff downtown. Perhaps you and I can go for a ride this afternoon."

"Ernest," she said, "someone opened a window last night. In here. During the storm."

He looked at her, face carefully blank, for several seconds. Tabatha rubbed her face.

"Are you sure you didn't—"

"I was asleep."

"Of course, of course," he said. "The wind perhaps? Or perhaps Amelia didn't secure them properly?"

She stared at him with an *almost* unfair amount of ice for his casual disregard. He squirmed in a satisfying way.

"I'll have a word with her," Tabatha said finally, then waved him on. "Send her up on your way out."

Amelia appeared moments later, her face blanched. Ernest must have given her too strong a word already.

"Now, now, Amelia," Tabatha said, "I know you would never

intentio—"

The Matron ignored her mistress and swept past to lean down into the bassinet. Morticia came up in her hands with a cry of surprised protest.

"Amelia!" Tabatha demanded, standing. "What in the name of the Lord—"

Amelia held the toddler at arms length, like she might a large rat caught in the pantry. Morticia's eyes snapped open and Amelia hissed. She thrust the child at Tabatha, who snatched her child to her breast with a glare for the Matron.

"AMELIA, *really!* What has gotten into you?!"

The woman stepped back, her mouth moved without a breath of sound. Her dry hands rasped as they rubbed sinuous circles around themselves. Finally, she spoke.

"I heard it from Elaine this morning... The winds and storm—an exchange—the witches—Elaine knew—well, she guessed, but she as good as knew—" The woman stammered to a halt beneath Tabatha's glare.

"Elaine knew what?" Tabatha asked over Morticia's feathery hair. "What, Amelia?"

"Well, she had it from someone else, of course, being Elaine—but they thought—they said that the witches—it's the witches seeking a third—they worried that a child—not just any child, one of their own—that this child might have... might have been... But not our Morticia, surely not! Surely not."

" 'SURELY NOT' WHAT?! DAMN YOU!"

Amelia hopped in place, her slippered feet creaking the hardwoods as she regained her balance. Tabatha's stomach had knotted itself to her spine once more. She knew where this led. She could feel it. Amelia cringed and contracted, hands rasping. Tabatha took a sharp, silent breath.

"Amelia, please."

"LOOK AT HER EYES, MUM!"

Tabatha continued to glare past her baby at the woman.

She steeled herself and raised Morticia up from her breast. The child opened its eyes. They were still blue, but solid orbs of translucent blue. Ice and snow. Ageless depth. The flecks of hazel were gone. *Wrong.* All wrong. Tabatha shuddered.

She placed the child back in the bassinet, tucking the blanket around it. It squirmed and mewled, then settled into a light sleep.

"What do you know?" she demanded softly.

Amelia had subsided into a fit of prayers, staring at the floor, hands rasping.

"Amelia, please." Tabatha reached out and touched the older woman's arm, sparking another small hop. "What is the meaning of this?"

"Please, mum, we... I think we have to let it be. If we tried to—that is to say—treating with witches—I mean, really. What would the Sheriff do?"

"Am—" Tabatha tried to interject, but Amelia rambled on.

"Hang us! Is what he'll do. Or burn us. Or worse!" She paced away. "Witches. Cursed witches. Why us? Why our Morticia?!"

"Amelia—"

"We can learn to love this one," the Matron went on, pacing back. "And she might—that is to say... They don't—they often don't last as—never reach past a certain age, that is. Changelings. And, and, and you're ready to bear another, anyway! We could have a little boy in the house. And Ernest-begging your pardon, Mr. Moresly-well forgive my saying so, but he'll not take much loss in the exchange..."

She trailed off, hands wringing each other blue and white. Trembling. Tabatha found that her chest felt tight. But her fists planted firm on her hips; just as Mother might have stood.

"What the devil are you talking about, woman?!" she demanded.

Amelia shuffled to a stop and looked at Tabatha.

"Precisely that, ma'am. I had it from Elaine this morning at the shop when I went 'round to pick up Mrs. Melanie's order like you asked. She went on and on about that horrible storm and devilry afoot and witches on the wind and 'a changeling got made in that evil wind' and 'a babe switched in the dark' and all manner of nonsense! But I worried anyway and I came straight home to check on her and... Well look, mum! *Look* at her eyes!"

Amelia finished in a fierce whisper then subsided once more into muttered prayers.

Tabatha looked down into the bassinet once more and the child looked back. Morticia's face, yes, but the eyes...

Tabath's bile rose and then her blood rose behind it. Someone, some*thing*, had taken her child. After a moment, the babe grinned, as if it knew the joke had run dry, but didn't care. Tabatha shuddered again, then steeled herself. She turned and grabbed Amelia's thick arms, giving the Matron a shake.

"Bundle it up and wait here for me," Tabatha told her. "And don't let Ernest..." *What?*

He wouldn't be back before nightfall and even then he'd never think to check on the child. Amelia had enough presence to nod her understanding.

Tabatha's dread built as she shut her front door. It clawed at her as she hesitated on the cobble stone street outside of their home. Someone had taken her child. Time felt fast and slippery. Her fingers twitched at her sides, as if eager to grab handfuls of the passing seconds and hold them down.

To her right, the street led away from the town center, toward Melanie's cottage on the outskirts of town.

To her left, Elaine's shop stood just around the corner. Much closer. Tabatha bit her lip. Time slipped by.

She shook herself and turned out toward Melanie's. She wanted her sister by her side for this.

After a few steps, Tabatha felt another cold rock tumble into her stomach. She slowed then stopped. Melanie and Charles had left. A business engagement or some such, two towns over. Her sister wouldn't return until the evening.

Alone, then. Drawing herself up, the mother turned back toward the dress shop, clutching her skirts to help keep her legs from sprinting through the streets.

. . .

The needle-headed seamstress, so quick to wag her tongue during a fitting, had proven downright recalcitrant when approached directly. Not even Elaine willingly discussed witches in the Sheriff's town. Melanie might have intimidated her more and dragged the information from her faster, but Tabatha got to it eventually. And, really, she didn't even regret threatening to beat the woman with one of her own corsets.

Cowering against the back wall of her store, Elaine offered the bits and pieces Tabatha needed: witches, the changeling, an exchange, the forest, moonlight.

Elaine, her wide eyes latched to the humanoid metal frame Tabatha wielded overhead, promised not to mutter a word of what she knew about the abduction to anyone else.

But this was Elaine. The explosion of lace and color in her shop served only to soften the sounds within. Whispers. The lush fabrics rustled loud enough to swallow up the tittered gossip of every house in town. Delectable scandals swam in these racks.

The Sheriff would hear about Morticia before sunset—but the witches wouldn't appear before moonrise. It would be a near thing.

. . .

Tabatha's skirts were in a state of ruin, muddied, drenched, and torn from traipsing through the snow-covered fields. She'd dropped her cloak somewhere along the way, but that didn't matter. Sweat drenched her garments. She felt the wind teasing the damp lanks of her hair into a mad-woman's halo. Tree branches moaned in the winter wind. The cold didn't bother Tabatha tonight any more than it ever had. Melanie would have turned back from these bitter winds an hour ago.

No, that did her too little credit. Melanie would have waded through slush and worse, to the far end of Creation for Morticia.

The wait through the day had nearly killed her. The changeling babe never cried, rarely stirred. It unnerved her. The silent house put jitters in her feet as she paced the halls, checking the sun minute after minute, urging it on. Amelia's muttered prayers trailed around the house behind her, punctured by sudden, curt swearing when a shadow or small noise startled her. Tabatha had come close to sending her home, but worried it would look too suspicious. She dreaded above all to hear a knock at the door and Amelia's shrill voice calling out, "Good day, Sheriff!"

He had not come. Neither had Ernest. The fool man stayed away and perhaps that was for the best. *Melanie.* She wanted Melanie.

Tabatha shook off all thoughts, focusing once more on the footpath squelching beneath her feet. Adjusting the bundle on her chest, she trudged on. Snow tickled her ankles and the wind howled. She cooed softly down to the babe, though the thing never stirred or complained.

The moon rose just as Tabatha's path intersected the Long Road. Across those snow-covered ruts, the forest loomed.

The wind took on a new pitch. It made the oaks of the old forest groan and creak as it wound through their twisted branches. Then it danced and rustled through the sparse growth of the young forest before sweeping out over the fields and roads of men. It whipped up Tabatha's hair and swirled around her.

A twist of wind hit the snowbank on the far side of the Long Road, sending a great cloud of crystalline powder billowing up. When the snow settled, two gaunt women stood on the far side of the road, their faces crooked and worn, sharp eyes glinting in the moonlight. Wild white hair hung limp from both their heads, still, despite the wind.

One stood tall and one lurked short.

The taller held a bundle to her chest. The sight curdled Tabatha's heart. She clutched the bundle against her own breast tighter. Sudden revulsion relaxed her grip again.

The young mother's gaze trailed down to the womens' feet. They stood *atop* the loose packed powder. *Witches.* They didn't have wands or broomsticks or heavy, hooded cloaks, but Tabatha felt their otherness in the moonlight. They stood two feet above her, perched impossibly on the fresh snowfall.

Tabatha opened her mouth to shout at the women and make her demand, but the tall one spoke first.

"You look like seven shades of—"

"the uglier side of Hell, girl."

"And few would know—"

"better than we."

They cackled in unison.

"It suits you," the tall one said with a toothy grin. Tabatha blinked, taken aback. The tall witch adjusted the bundle and grinned wider. Rage surged.

"I've come for Morticia!" Tabatha shouted.

Both women raised their eyebrows, then exchanged a quick grin.

"We can't return to you what—"

"was never yours, child."

The shorter one spat to the side, then smirked at Tabatha.

"Is that or is that not my child?" Tabatha demanded.

"'Twas ne'er yours—" the tall witch stated, tickling Morticia's nose.

"nor was she ours."

"Her life's her own—"

"as well her powers be."

The witches both glanced over Tabatha's head, back toward the town.

"Your time wanes—"

"as hers waxes."

Tabatha whipped around. Miles of snow covered fields stretched back to the squat stone buildings and steep roofs. Candlelit windows flickered in the dark. A gust of wind slapped at her head, wrapping sweat damp hair around her eyes. She swept it back with a shaking hand. Two dark shapes shrouded in thin clouds of steam forged up the snowy lane. Clouds shifted and moonlight revealed the silhouettes of two horses leaving the candle lights behind. The Sheriff and, Tabatha hoped, Ernest.

Tabatha clutched the babe tight to her chest and turned back to the witches—who stood at their ease, watching the horses approach.

Morticia gave a tiny cry. Tabatha felt something crumble inside.

"Your hours grow thin—"

"and your minutes precarious. Ask—"

"the question."

Tabatha's breath shallowed. Her mind raced.

"But we don't have— We're not— She's just a child. An infant! Will you not return her? For this one? An even exchange?"

"Wrong—"

"question,"

"dearie."

"Ask," the witches said together. Their voices echoed despite the soft snow all around.

Tabatha stared.

"What do you *want?!*" Tabatha shouted.

The witches grinned at her in unison.

"We two—"

"must be three."

"Three covens—"

"three valleys."

"Three and three—"

"shall we ever be."

Wind whipped across the hills and down the road. Tiny dervishes of snow raced past and dissipated in shadow.

"I don't understand!" Tabatha said. "Give her back, please!" Something raw and weak tore up her throat and she screamed the word again. "Please! ... please—please." She sobbed.

"Oh it's 'please' now—"

"is it?! Still not so—"

"pleasing to the ear."

They laughed. It sounded to Tabatha like the crackling of dead branches. A numbness seeped through her. Her eyes drifted up, into the dark woods beyond the witches. Trees swayed in the breeze, but the cold wind never touched her.

Had never touched her. *Nor Morticia. She's never shivered.* The tall one had turned the bundle around, sitting Moriticia's rump on a bony forearm and letting her look out. Her child did not cry.

"Three..." Tabatha said.

"and three—"

"shall we ever—"

"be," she finished.

The tall witch swayed with Morticia in her arms. Her face softened around the eyes.

"Your mother left these woods—"

"and none return—"

"from where she's gone."

"Yet her line—"

"her blood—"

"runs on."

"Our blood runs on—"

"and on—"

"forever." They finished together.

The wind shifted and Tabatha caught the pounding of hoofbeats behind her. She swore, then ripped her hungry eyes away from her babe. Two torches. Two men. The bold hat of the Sheriff and a flash of green, Ernest's favorite riding cloak.

"Eternal damnation on all gossips," she swore again, turning back to face the witches.

The wind nipped at them, then swiped snow up the hill in a cresting wave. As it fell, they disappeared.

"No!" Tabatha lunged forward, tripping on her skirts and fumbling the changeling. She recovered and clutched it tight to her chest, hunched over in the middle of the Long Road. Alone.

She heard the snort of a horse behind her and turned just as the riders sawed their reins at the end of the path.

"Tabatha!" Ernest cried out, leaping down. He threw clouds of snow-dust up as he strode to her. "What in heaven's name are you doing out here? And who are these wom—" He stopped, brows knitting.

The Sheriff sat tall in his saddle, scanning the road, the hills, and the forest with flat eyes.

"Where did they go?" Ernest asked. "The women on the hill?"

"Witches," the Sheriff said, dismounting. He planted his feet and unbuttoned his coat. A hatchet hung on a bandolier across his chest, its silver edge sparking. He wrapped a gloved hand around its worn handle and slid it free. "Tabatha Edgecomb Moresly you hereby stand accused of witchcraft."

A breeze whistled between them, rising and then fading back into the woods.

"Witchcraft?! Don't be daft!" Ernest blurted, voice straining through a tight throat. His head swiveled all around the landscape. There was no sign of the women. Tabatha felt a chill. She cooed to the child and bounced it on her chest.

"A trick of the moonlight, Sheriff! They were just—women, out for a stroll—after dark—on the edge of the... woods..."

His eyes darted through the moonlit trees, piercing the snow as if to give shape to the shadows.

Ernest finally turned back to his wife and down to the bundle at her chest. He seemed confused, perhaps, even, betrayed. Tabatha couldn't stop the fear spreading through her leaden limbs now, couldn't help looking at him with a horrified plea in her eyes.

Ernest blinked and turned to the Sheriff.

"Don't be daft..."

The Sheriff stood still, watching them, hatchet hanging loose at his side. He stood with the straight-backed pride of a man accepting the necessity of an unclean task. His gaze held neither fear nor accusation. He took a step toward Tabatha.

Ernest stepped between them, his hand out, fingertips resting on the

Sheriff's hatchet hand.

"I need no further proof," the Sheriff said, looking past Ernest. "She convenes with the witches."

"What do you intend?"

Tabatha felt a sudden, surprising well of affection for her husband. The Sheriff darted a glance at Ernest's face before returning to her.

"Tonight: the dungeon with a guard," the Sheriff said. "Tomorrow: a trial at first light. She will burn at the stake in innocence before God or prove her guilt by surviving."

He twitched the hatchet, flashing the silver-edged blade.

Tabatha felt nothing. No fear. No anger. She thought that she should, but nothing came. She watched Ernest's shoulders bunch up, ready to fight. The Sheriff didn't tense, but his flat eyes turned to her husband. Tabatha's heart pounded in her chest, blood flowed in her arms.

Ernest's shoulders slumped. The force fell from him and his finger-tips slid from the Sheriff's hand. A shot of dread fell down Tabatha's backbone as he turned to her. The broad-chested fool worked to keep his face neutral, holding out his hands for the child, casting her aside without a word.

"The child stays here," the Sheriff said. "With the witches. I'll have none of their ilk in my town."

Ernest's face twitched toward anger, outrage, for a moment, but then fell back into the abyss. His arms fell back to his sides. It prickled Tabatha, beyond hope or reason, she gripped the child close to her.

"Preposterous!" Tabatha shouted. "Leave an infant in the snow?! Alone?!"

"I believe it to be a changeling," the Sheriff said, straightforward. "Devilry from the witches. Did you trade your own child for occult powers? The promise of a son? What deal did you make with them?"

Tabatha glared at him over the baby's head. The wind howled and branches cracked in the woods. She thought she heard an old woman's cackle, just around the edges of the forest. She clutched the babe tight. It had all turned in on them so quickly. *Morticia.*

She glanced at her husband, master and protector of his great house. He studied a point just over her head.

"Ernest," she said. He ignored her. "Ernest, please..." Her voice cracked. She hated that. His gaze fell to the snow at his feet. She shivered.

Tabatha strode forward, shouldering Ernest aside. The Sheriff jerked his hatchet up, but she stopped short to push the baby under his nose Sheriff's face.

"Look at her! Look! She's just an infant. A child!"

The Sheriff glanced at the snowbank, then back to Tabatha. He dropped his hatchet, letting it hang on a leather thong around his wrist. Gently, he pulled the child from her arms, holding it out as if its touch might burn. She relented, slowly. The babe had woken up and stared back at him with pale blue eyes. Perfect and harmless, swaddled in her bundle.

"You see?" Tabatha asked. "It's just a child. Let her go. Please."

The Sheriff hesitated, staring at the babe. He grunted.

"My sister could take—"

THe Sheriff hoisted the infant up overhead, then hurled the bundle toward the woods. The swaddling cloth twisted idly in the moonlight as the bundle sailed over the road. Tabatha screeched and leapt after it, but the Sheriff hooked her elbow and swung her back, down to the hard ground, a knee into her back.

Tabatha fought and screamed as the Sheriff tied her wrists behind her back. He ripped a strip of fabric from her dress and made to gag her, but she hissed and bit at him. He jerked a hand from her snapping teeth with a grunt, then gave her a sharp slap. She reeled toward the ground but stood again immediately, her head spinning. He hit her once more, then again when she stood back up. She doubled over and spat bloody phlegm into the white snow. He shoved the muddy rag in her mouth and cinched it at the base of her neck.

He pulled her upright. His face hadn't changed. A man doing an unsavory duty. Neither enjoying the task, nor hating her. Simply protecting his town.

Ernest stood rooted where she'd left him, gazing at her with an open mouth. She looked at the hole in the snow where the infant, the changeling, had disappeared. Now the pain came, crumpling her from within.

Ernest shut his mouth, mounted his horse, and rode. He did not look back.

The Sheriff watched him go, then gave his head a sad shake. "Now, Mrs. Moresly, you can ride in front of me, quietly. Let me help you—"

She leapt forward and headbutted him, catching his nose with her forehead. The bone gave a satisfying crunch. He swore and staggered back, blowing blood from both nostrils. A red patch blossomed and grew in the snow at his feet. Eventually, he stood up, clenching his nose and grimacing at her. His hand had found the hatchet handle again, but he swept the other arm up instead. The backhanded slap caught her across the temple. She spun, crying out, and fell to the frozen path.

He picked her up and hoisted her over the back of his horse, then mounted up in front of her and they set off. Dazed, she watched the snow bank recede, bobbing as the horse's rump flexed.

Moonlight glinted on the powder, shadowing the divot in the bank. Rage bubbled up for her now, rage in a thousand different flavors. A sharp wind rose, pelting her face with ice and stinging her bruised cheek. As she winced, the gust whipped past the snowbank and a brilliant puff of powder shot up from the hole where the child had disappeared. The cloud twisted and gleamed in the moonlight. It stuck to itself in fits and clumps, condensing and taking shape.

A raven, stark white feathers glinting in the moonlight, flapped its wings and disappeared among the stars.

· · ·

Her cell had a barred window at head height which opened to a muddy alley behind the jail. She'd curled up on the stone floor where they'd thrown her, and not moved for hours. A tiny puddle of tears had frozen beneath her face. A tattered blanket lay in the corner. She ignored it. The cold seeping from the walls did not touch her, but her swollen cheek throbbed.

Tabatha sank to the stone floor and cried quietly. She drifted. The stone floor felt cool on her cheek, then cold.

In the quiet dark, she saw the witches, disappearing from the snowy hill. She saw Morticia and the tall witch and her knowing grin. The short witch lurking at her side. The two who must be three. Ernest, staring over her head. The bundle, unraveling in the air. Raven on the wing. Snow on the wind.

She heard droplets, falling to water below. A tiny, endless, dripping rhythm.

Then, a hiss among the drips. A water droplet landed in flames. Another. Another.

A taste like metal clipped at her breath. She stood in a cave. Ice rose from the floor and dangled overhead. A flame bloomed before her, its thousands of tongues lashing up at the icicles. The ice dripped, but did not melt. The steam rose, but did not freeze. The flame stuttered in the droplets, but would never go out.

tink tink tink

Something tapped on the bars of the window. The vision slipped away. Tabatha groaned.

tink tink tink

She raised her chin and wiped her face. The white raven perched between the bars, head cocked to show her one bright blue orb.

It cawed and bobbed its head, nodding her over to the window. She groaned, then shut her eyes again and curled back around her pain. Snores rattled down the hall.

tink tink tink

tink tink tink

Tabatha dragged herself to her knees, grunting at the pain. She shuffled to the wall and slid up to rest her head by the window. She felt the weight of her bones. Every bit of her ached.

The raven gave a soft caw, then leaned in next to her ear. She felt a puff of breath and heard the snip of its beak.

"Well, you look terrible." The voice sounded low but clear. A male voice, with a touch of mischief to it. She knew she should have felt shocked or awed, but pain and loss had burned through her. A shell.

"I ate an apple as bruised as you once, upset my stomach for a whole day."

"Why are you here, changeling?" Tabatha replied in a monotone. "The witches would gloat over my living corpse? Do they watch through your eyes? Feed on my pain?"

"Ahhhh," the raven said, "Self-pitying and morbid. A sourpuss. Auspicious opening."

Tabatha felt nothing, said nothing. She gazed back down into her cell.

"Well!" he chirruped. "I come with hope; an alternative to burning at the stake, for the sourpuss." Tabatha rolled her head around to look at him.

"From the witches?"

"From the witches—" the raven repeated, "after a fashion, yes." He gave one short caw. The guard snorted. Tabatha tensed, but she heard a creak of leather as he settled himself. He slept on.

"I'm here for you, sourpuss. That's the important thing, really. So, how about a smile?"

Without thought, Tabatha's hand shot out and she caught the mouthy bastard by his throat. It choked out a small caw and beat its wings against her arm. She squeezed, it choked. A wild burst of feathers, a tiny popping sound, and a mouse skittered up her arm to her neck. She slapped at it, but it leapt back out the window. Another pop and the raven glided down to land a few feet away. A wave of gray sunlight crept up its wings as it glared at her, clicking its beak.

"Violent," it said, finally. "Reminds me of your mother."

The raven hopped back toward the window, just out of her reach. Tabatha stared at it.

"My mother?"

"Sure."

"You knew her?"

"Better than you."

Tabatha's hand itched to snap at it again. It skipped back. She sighed.

"Why? Tell me why. Why Morticia?" *Why me?*

The raven shrugged.

"The blood runs on and on; we can only follow." It shrugged its wings.

"Damn your riddles!" She slammed the bar with a fist.

Her shout and the clang echoed up the stone walls.

The guard's snores hitched and faltered—then resumed.

The cell felt quieter.

"Look at me," said the raven.

Tabatha turned to him, stared at the one large eye directed her way. It spread its wings wide.

"You're being an idiot," he said.

Her eyes narrowed of their own accord. She turned her back on him.

"Listen and understand. You and your daughter. You both have a right to the magic. You tug the power back and forth between you, unknowing. One of you must take it. One of you *will* take it."

Outside the cell, the oil lamp flickered. Orange light played on the bars. Gentle snores echoed up the hall.

"Why not you?" it asked.

The air tasted sharp. Tabatha shook her head.

"Because she's safe. She's cared for. I don't need—anything else."

The raven waited. Tabatha hunched over herself, felt the warmth of her own breath leaving her lungs.

"I don't. I don't need it. I don't need to—not if she's safe. Is she safe?"

"Yes, but—"

"That's all that matters. She's all that matters."

"Mmm."

Columns of ice. Endless flame.

She breathed. In the distance, she could just make out the sound of dripping water. The hiss of steam.

"Are you... absolutely sure about that?" the raven asked.

"Mrs. Moresly!"

A winking eye, a burst of feathers, a puff of snow. The raven slipped between the wan rays of moonlight and disappeared.

Amelia trundled to a halt, frozen and staring up the alley. She had bundled up against the cold, layers of cloaks and dresses covering every inch of her squat frame. She lowered her pile of fabrics to the stones by the barred window, falling forward to grasp the iron with gloved hands.

"Where is—I came just as soon—Oh my LORD the state of—What's he done to your face! I've sent for—Did you— Morticia?!"

Her breath gushed and gurgled, misting the air between them.

Tabatha reached up and put her hands over Amelia's.

"Who did you send for?"

"Miss Melanie, of course."

No. Tabatha's heart clenched. Amelia continued.

"Ernest-beg your pardon-Mr. Moresly was in a snit. And I had word that Melanie-beg your pardon-Mrs. Whitten had got home late. I hope you'll forgive me over-reaching, it's just that Mr. Moresly came home in *such* a snit! Wouldn't say a decent word to me! And you didn't come home at all! And I didn't know who else to call on, not having much sway with the Sheriff myself, of course. So, Melanie-beg your pardon-Mrs. Whitten will be along shortly to sort all this."

Tabatha gripped the bar of the cell tightly and stared out at the moonlit stones in the alley. She'd hoped to disappear. The rest of the town could watch her burn and be damned. But Melanie. Melanie would lose so much so quickly. A hardness crept under Tabatha's ribs; snaking vines constricting, clenching tight around her heart. Each beat hurt more than the last. *She can't... she can't be here... she can't see this... I can't... I can't...* Her cowardice twisted those vines all the tighter.

"Amelia-" Tabatha's voice came up small and choked. The matron shuffled her pile of cloth and adjusted her knees, unhearing.

"Witchcraft! Ooo he's gone 'round the bend this time. The Sheriff. *Hmph!* And Ernest-beg your pardon-that... Ooo. *Men.* I mean we've all known the Edgecomb girls to be—to have a bit of—" She snapped her mouth shut, then ran on. "But *witches?!*"

Amelia's eye caught on Tabatha's bare fingers wrapped around the iced bars of the window.

"Oh Miss! You must be frozen stiff! Take one of these—"

"No, keep it, Amelia," Tabatha said, without thinking. She snapped her hands off the bars. "I'm fine."

Amelia froze with a cloak halfway off her back, staring at Tabatha's hands. She swallowed hard. The stout woman's exhales crystallized in the moonlight between them. Tabatha's breath hardly misted the air at all.

"Do you—that is—what will happen, mum?" Her voice lowered. "Tomorrow morning I mean? Will they—will you—"

Ice above, fire below.

Tabatha stared at her fingers, veins standing up on their backs; they tingled.

From one heartbeat to the next, Tabatha's chest felt light, lighter than the snow, than the rays of the moon.

"I don't know."

The guard around the corner snored fitfully. Amelia started.

The guard around the corner snored fitfully. Amelia started.

"Miss..." Amelia whispered. "I think—uhm—that is—" She adjusted her cloaks and started to rise.

Tabatha snaked a hand out and gently grabbed the Matron's wrist.

"You have family, Amelia, in Taunton?"

Amelia froze again.

"Yes, ma'am. Though I haven't seen them in quite some time."

"Perhaps you should join them for an early breakfast tomorrow?"

"Mum...?"

"And perhaps stay over for a longer visit?"

"Won't Mr. Moresly—"

"Mr. Moresly can cook his own breakfast and then rot in hell."

Amelia blinked.

"I see. Well... I... should be going then."

"Thank you, Amelia." She let go and turned away.

A strong, stubby hand slipped through the bars to grab her shoulder. Tabatha felt a warm caress of breath and as the matron whispered a short, fierce prayer on the back of her ear. The hand slipped away and Tabatha sat in silence, watching the flicker of the oil lamp across the hall.

Ice froze and dripped. Fire ebbed and rose.

The blood runs on and on... forever.

Time passed. Tabatha rested, eyes fluttering shut, watching the duet ice and fire.

"Tabatha!" Melanie called.

The witch smiled. She turned to greet her sister.

"I've told Charles, he's penning a petition to the Sheriff. Oh! But this damn thing pinches for no good reason, confound it! Why are you laughing?!"

Tabatha couldn't help it. The weight of the world had lifted from her so quickly, the relief dragged her head up to clouds and left her light. She giggled as her sister adjusted and readjusted the corset so that she could kneel in the snow.

Melanie glared at her.

"I'm sorry, sister," She bit her fist to still the laughter in her chest. "You're right, of course, I shouldn't— We're not free of this yet."

"No, but we will be. Charles is also writing an appeal that he'll send to an old friend in the morning; some stodgy judge over in Boston, progressive type. We'll have some common sense in this town if I have to beat it into everyone myself."

Tabatha smiled fondly at her sister.

"What? What is it?"

"I'm grateful," she said. "Truly"

"You should be. I put this foolish torture device on for you, you know? Charles couldn't believe it, his sister-in-law accused of occult practices and his wife stuffing herself into this wagonload of ivory and metal. He started writing immediately."

"That won't—" Tabatha caught herself and stopped. None of this was Melanie's fault. "Thank you. But that will not be necessary."

"Tabby, you have to let us help you," Melanie said, slow and direct. The calm of fear. "And where is Ernest?"

They shared a look. Tabatha's eyes fell to the floor. Melanie reached out and lifted her sister's face, gently running a finger over her bruised cheek.

"Do I need to have him poisoned?"

"What?! No, Melanie, let him be. Let him go. We have to help ourselves, to do what's best for Morticia."

She regretted the words almost immediately.

"What?! Why? Where is she?" Melanie's eyes darted around the cell as if she expected the baby to be lying unattended in a corner of the jail. "The Sheriff didn't—"

"No. He would have, though. That's what matters. She's safe. For now. The witches have her."

Melanie gasped, flapping her mouth open and shut, no doubt ready to beat some sense into the witches as well, or else to poison them.

"How do we—"

"We don't," Tabatha cut in. "The witches only want one of us."

"One of who?! For what?!"

"To replace Mother."

They shared another long look.

"No—"

"We are what we are, Melanie."

"Then I'll go," her sister said, nodding. "Of course I will. I'll go and you'll get Morticia back. And I'll turn the Sheriff and Ernest into toads so they can't get you ever again."

Tabatha smiled and put her hand over her sisters.

"I know you would, but you can't," she said.

They talked for some time. Melanie protested often and loudly.

Tabatha persisted quietly. The guard snored.

The gray of dawn had filtered into the alley when they finally hugged and kissed through the bars, tears mingling with the ice.

When Melanie left, she went hunched forward over her grief and frustration. She kicked the snow out of her path with purpose all the long way back to their small house.

The witch sank to the floor of her cell. She smiled, picturing the cave, the flickering flames, the dripping ice.

A sudden gust of cold wind blew a cloud of snow through the window.

When the snow fell, the witch was gone.

• • •

Melanie woke slowly. Streaks of morning light shot through the cracked curtains of their cottage window.

Tabatha.

She'd slept fitfully. Awfully. In bed beside her, Charles' back rose and fell with each gentle breath. She'd come home to find him feverishly penning an appeal that would never be sent. He hadn't understood, or, rather, hadn't believed a word of it. But — with some coaxing — he had put the pen down and packed up their carriage. They were ready.

A sudden spark of thought lit on her. She'd... had a dream. *The* dream. So real she could still feel the crisp touch where a snowflake had landed on her cheek. She touched her face and found a damp spot. Had she wept?

Morticia.

Groggy but purposeful, she rose from her bed, found her robe in the dusky light and padded out without waking Charles.

She went straight to the front door of their cottage. The dream... she had to know. Melanie ripped the door open, the sunlight glared down on the fresh snow on the fields around their cottage, blinding her. She threw an arm up to shield her eyes.

A basket, nestled in the snow on their front porch. A small, pink nose poked up from up from bundles of blue cloth.

Morticia. The babe lay swaddled and content, staring up at her.

Melanie cried out and snatched the child up to her chest. Morticia's face felt cold, even through her nightgown. Melanie began to rub at her back. She squinted, searching the surrounds for signs of Tabatha. At first, she saw only rolling banks of snow and the white capped roofs of the town in the distance.

Then on a snowbank half the distance back to town, wind whipped up a billowing cloud and three shadows stood atop the snow. Melanie stared at them, open mouthed.

The wind turned and the cloud dissipated, shadows disappearing in the rising daylight.

Morticia nuzzled at Melanie's neck.

Cooing to the child — and hastily wiping tears on the shoulder of her nightdress — Melanie darted inside the cottage to wake her husband. They had a long journey ahead.

Woah there Space Cowboy

A bold supporter of this work hopes
you'll take a moment to ponder and
revel in our contribution to the stars

Of Art
by Tessa

Artists act as a parent to
society, ready to pick them up
and weather the tantrums as
they stumble down a path of
life

Art is born of desire while science is
born of necessity, together they
capture the best of innovation
humanity has to offer

Artists hold a mirror to the face of
society and wait with baited
breath as society decides whether
or not it likes what it sees

If art is the product of an artist's
soul, to sit in judgment of art is to
take the god's power as your own

Vigiles Fungorum

Introduction

Mushrooms. The beautiful, dangerous delicacies of the wood-lands.They bloom, sprout, pop-up, and protrude from the decomposing bio-litter of every temperate forest in the world, offering a tender bite for the curious, brave, and well-informed forager.

Millenia ago, humans discovered the bounty within the Kingdom Fungi and, through precise scientific experimentation, we learned to protect ourselves from indigestion and accidental poisoning.

That is to say, thousands of foolish and intrepid foragers suffered a ridiculous amount of indigestion and accidental poisonings in order to write field guides for the layman.

Thanks to their sacrifice, we can, as of this writing, accurately identify and safely consume over 2,000 varieties of the forest's most succulent treats. A litany of well-crafted and highly detailed field guides exist to keep foragers safe in their pursuit of these morsels.

And yet, I feel compelled to add my own text to this already ample pile of information.

A host of other-worldly beings and phenomena take refuge in the shaded stalks of the Kingdom Fungi. In my travels and explorations, I have made extensive notes on the non-human sentinels and forces that guard our forests' mushrooms. As I leafed through other texts and field guides, I found the information in this extranormal realm to be rather thin.

Though most are harmless, a handful pose a real threat to amateur and experienced foragers alike.

Where the mushroom's natural defenses of simple camouflage and outright poisons have serious implications for the human forager, these challenges often pale in comparison to those posed by the myriad Sentinels of the Forest.

In my travels I have been burned, scorned, hoodwinked, poisoned, burned again, teleported, insulted, burned once more for luck, and, of course, richly rewarded.

If the only words you retained from the last sentence were "richly rewarded", then I can guarantee that your fingers will be scorched often and severely.

I offer to you now a field guide that encapsulates both the physical characterizations which serve as the mushroom forager's lifeblood, alongside my own brief notes on the "Fantastical Elements" that you may encounter in your expeditions. These notes include my advice on avoiding the myriad perils of spiritual forces, exotic creatures, and grumpy guardians.

My deep and heartfelt gratitude goes out to the authors, editors, and gatherers who helped publish A Field Guide to Mushrooms of the Carolinas, from which many observations were liberally borrowed.

Also many thanks to the editors Hunter Gatherer magazine for featuring this excerpt of Vigiles Fungorum.

So then. Till next we meet, tread lightly, snack wisely, and never forget to enjoy and appreciate the simple peace of immersion in nature.

. . .

Yellow Morel
Morchella americana

Description:
Fruitbody 4–22 cm tall (occasionally much larger). Head 2–11 cm high and 1.5–4cm wide, usually oval or cylindrical, a busy network of randomly arranged ridges and pits. Flesh brittle.

Occurrence:
Spring. Scattered, in groups or clusters under ash or elm or in apple orchards, also with other hardwoods, near streams, or with conifers.

Edibility:
Choice, but must be cooked.

Spore Print:
Ochre

Microscopic Features:
Spores 17–24 x 11–15 µm, elliptic

Fantastical Elements:
Creature. Highly dangerous.
Occasionally host djinn within a vaporous smoke derived from the Plains of Essence.

A. Kerns Comments:

Known to some foresters as the "Towers of the Djinni", Morels appear in cool, damp climates toward mid-spring. Look for their heads to protrude just above thick leaf-litter in groves of oak, elm, ash, and aspen trees. Even seasoned foragers feel proud to spot them and twice lucky if the morel they harvest happens to free a djinni. (Fig. 1)

The djinni will appear from the largest morel in a growth, hidden within a miasma of smoke that's shot through with specks of dark ash and twinkling lights (echoes of the Planes of Essence from which they're temporarily banished). The smoke binds them; lean close to note the shadowy figure near the center revealing their trapped essence.

Keep in mind, the powers of the djinni have diminished greatly over the years. You'll likely receive just one wish and a small one at that. Negotiate firmly, but fairly. The djinni will be motivated—granting your wish frees them to return to the spirit plane. Foragers be warned, however: djinni have a devious relationship with words and a twisted wit. A poorly phrased wish could scar or even kill you.

Black Trumpets
Craterellus fallax

Description:
Cap 8 cm wide, deeply funnel-shaped. Margin inrolled at first, becoming uplifted and wavy or lobed. Grayish to dark brown or blackish. Lower surface similarly colored or paler, often with orange tints.

Occurrence:
Spring. Scattered, in groups or clusters often in moss banks under hardwoods or mixed woods. Late spring – fall.

Edibility:
Choice.

Spore Print:
Pale pinkish-orange.

Microscopic Features:
Spores 11–14 x 7–9 µm, broadly elliptic, smooth. Hyaline.

Fantastical Elements:
Creature. Dangerous. The Volcano Salamander's ear is a look-alike for the Black Trumpet; acidic excretions from the ear can fly up to 10 inches; acid will burn skin on contact.

A. Kerns Comments:

A tender trophy! Delicious in cream sauces and even atop a fresh salad. Look for these beauties through late summer, when they'll sprout in small batches at the bases of white oak trees. Of course, such a tasty treat doesn't come without a bit of risk! Enter: the Volcano Salamander. (Fig. 2)

A lingering ancestor to the great amphibious dragons of old, these tiny descendants still pack an almighty wallop for the uncautious mushroom forager.

A full-grown Volcano Salamander ear looks exactly like a black trumpet mushroom and they use the acorns of these oaks to help brew a wicked acid. Unlike their vibrant, harmless cousin the Fire Salamander, the Volcano Salamander sports a cloak of muted blacks, reds, and browns, a seamless blend for the forest floor. They sleep under cover of fallen leaves, but keep an ear up to listen for danger and lure in prey.

Tug on a Salamander's ear with a bare hand and you can expect to enjoy nasty blisters for several weeks. They can spew acid up to ten inches and just a drop will scorch any exposed skin. Note also that a tincture of lavender buds, calendula flowers, and chamomile can help cool the resulting boils and ease the discomfort.

Only a greedy and impatient harvester goes after a Trumpet which stands alone. Look for clusters of mushrooms instead and wear long gloves if you wish to avoid a light scorching.

Golden Chanterelles
Canthatellus tenuithrix

Description:
Cap typically 4–7 cm wide, inrolled at first, often lobed or wavy and uplifted in age. Upper surface dry, egg yellow to bright orange. Lower surface similarly colored decurrent gill-like ridges. Stalk 18–26 mm long, 7–10 mm thick, nearly equal, whitish to pale yellow. Odor like apricots.

Occurrence:
Solitary, scattered, or in groups. In or near woods. Late spring to fall.

Edibility:
Choice.

Spore Print:
Pale cream.

Microscopic Features:
Spores 78–.5 x 3.5–4.5 μm, elliptic or peanut-shaped, smooth.

Fantastical Elements:
Creature. Moderately dangerous. Often hilarious. Chanterelle Sprites are known for lude behavior, brick-headed obstinacy, and ludicrous insults. Mind their tempestuous personalities, their potent cantrips of confusion, and the sting of their small fireballs.

A. Kerns Comments:
A well-known and contentious favorite of chefs and forest sprites. Sprites tend toward non-violence, but don't raise their ire. Though tiny, sprite's cantrips have left many humans bruised, burnt, or terribly brain-addled for days.

If you meet a sprite near a patch of Chanterelles (Fig. 3), politely ask permission to harvest, and don't press your luck. Plan to also collect some creative, verbose insults. Sprites cannot swear, but make up for it by going to extraordinary lengths to offend hikers and foragers. Recently, I was referred to as "the flea-bitten buttcheek of a dead goat's mold-ridden rump."

However, by maintaining your composure and showing unflappable respect for the sprites and the woods they inhabit, you stand to make a fierce new friend.

A final word of advice: don't push sprites too far or too fast for information on Chanterelles. They guard that knowledge closely and their small fireballs will raise quite a welt.

Lion's Mane (Bearded Tooth; Satyr's Beard)

Hericium erinaceus

Description:
Fruitbody up to 20 cm high and white, a whitish to yellowish cushion-shaped mass giving rise to long spines and resembling a beard. Spines up to 9 cm long, white. Flesh thick, soft, white. Odor and taste not distinctive when young, becoming sour and unpleasant in age.

Occurrence:
Solitary or in groups on trunks, logs, and stumps of decaying hardwood trees. Summer–early winter.

Edibility:
Edible.

Spore Print:
White.

Microscopic Features:
Spores 5–6.5 x 4–5.6 µm, oval to globose, smooth to slightly roughened, Hyaline.

Fantastical Elements:
Phenomenon. Highly dangerous. Some foragers report disappearing from one location and reappearing several feet away, while others find themselves hundreds of miles away. Regrettably, some would-be harvesters of the Lion's Mane disappear and do not return.

A. Kerns Comments:

Witnesses compare the moment to stop-motion animation. One moment, their compatriot reaches out to touch the Lion's Mane mushroom, the next they disappear.

Most often foragers reappear nearby, dangling from low-hung tree branches or flat on their backs in piles of manure. #RideTheLion made light sport of touching this mushroom, until a series of deaths and disappearances caught the public by surprise.

This author's heart goes out to the families of those who've lost loved ones to this silly trend. I implore you all now to only approach this mushroom only out of dire necessity. We understand very, very little of the phenomena at play behind this innocent fungus; not even to say if it is sentient. Ongoing research hopes to unlock the secrets of this apparent faster-than-light travel for the good of mankind. Perhaps then, the succulent meat of the Lion's Mane will return to our dinner plates.

Until such a time, however, I urge the utmost caution and a clear life insurance policy for would-be foragers of the Lion's Mane. One who rides the lion may travel far and never return.

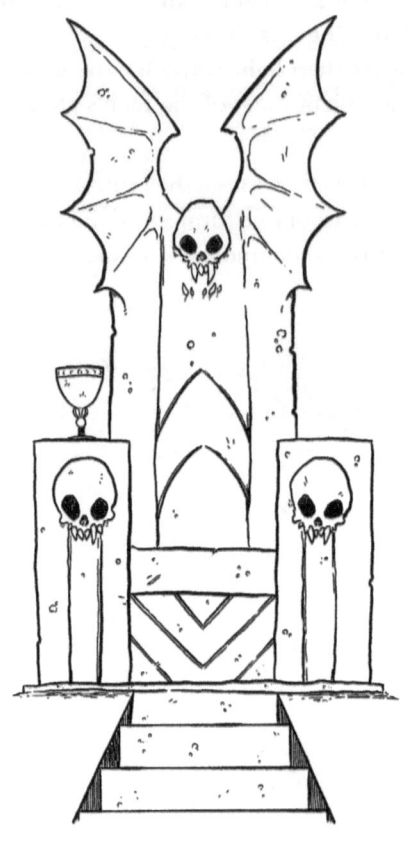

To Have and to Hold

Officer Rodriguez sat down at 7 am, placing his coffee and his chive cream cheese bagel on the precinct's reception desk.

At the desk, he knew to expect a slew of trivial and irritating crap. But. The idiocy usually didn't start before eight or so. Which meant that he could savor a slow breakfast.

The springy scent of chive wafted up as the officer peeled back the bagel's aluminum blanket. Still warm and soft from the toasting. He smiled and raised the bagel to his mouth.

The door chime tinkled.

Rodriguez's eyes shot open and he watched a teenage girl skulk into the precinct. He froze with the bagel an inch from his lips. The girl hunched under a heavy backpack and the bags under her eyes shined darkly in the fluorescents. A highschool junior or senior with a small build. He didn't recognize her, which was usually a good sign. He set the bagel down (sighing his lament) and waited for her to reach the desk.

She drew herself up in front of him, sniffed in a breath, then let words pour out.

"Good morning. My name is Emmie and I would like to file a restraining order against a classmate," the girl said. Quiet and self-assured, but shaky.

His heart sank. He'd missed it in his first pass, the crumpling, the fragility, the hunted look. Should have caught that.

"Good morning, Emmie. I'm Officer Rodriguez. I've got that form right here. You and the person in question, both students at Elmwood High?"

"Yes, sir," she said. Her eyes glittered. Actually fucking glittered. Hope like that didn't belong in a police station. And he'd have to be the one to crush her hopes. Stupid front desk.

"Okay," he said, "so why the restraining order? This guy–uhm–person—touch you?"

"Yes," she said, instantly. "Oh, I mean. No. Not, uhm, sexually. If that's what you meant." She hesitated for a moment, then let it all pour out. "Not overtly sexual. Not yet. He just—he won't leave me alone. He's always watching. He follows me at school, brings me things

I don't want, joined all my clubs, knows my route home, he's ruining everything, he's—" she sucked in a breath to continue the gush, but Rodriguez held up his hands.

"Hey now, easy there," he said. "We can work on that." The truth, but covering a thin lie. He glanced down at the bagel, cooling and hardening on his desk, and bit back the frustrated sigh.

Emmie nodded and turned to pull something out of her backpack. Rodriguez's suspicious right hand strayed toward his holster—but she came up with a notebook. He relaxed and took it with his gun hand.

"I've been recording it all," she said. "For the last year."

His eyebrows bumped up a notch.

"You mind if I take a look?"

She shook her head, then started filling out the Elmwood DD11 Restraining Order Request Form.

He opened the notebook to the first page and started to decipher her pen scratches. Each entry had a date scribbled above it, and they all started with the name Peter.

Peter Andrews met me at my house and walked me to school, talked about "us" the whole way.

...

Peter got us two tickets to the movies this Friday. I won't be going.

...

Peter brought me a birthday present. A terrible bottle of perfume and a promise ring. I threw both away. He's getting worse.

He flipped through the pages, observing the boy's spiral into obsession.

Peter showed up...

Peter watched me...

Peter followed...

Peter put his hand on my shoulder in the cafeteria today. His eyes looked all wrong. Hungry and desperate and disgusting. I ran and hid in the bathroom until fourth period. Need to get Bio notes from Shelby.

...

Peter's Red Schwinn Bike outside my house tonight. Too scared to go look for him in the yard, but sure he's here. Dad won't be home for a while.

...

Rodriguez noted that four of the last ten entries centered on the girl's home. But the other six happened at school. His stomach soured.

He shut the book and placed it on the desk.

"I need to go check on something," Rodriguez told her, standing. "Just fill that out and I'll be back in a minute."

She glanced over her shoulder, then back up to him. Him in his dark, pressed uniform. His shield. His gun. She nodded.

Rodriguez made to leave, but caught a glint of motion at the door. Another kid, walking a red bike past the window. He glared out and Emmie turned.

"He's here..." she whispered.

"You're safe," he told Emmie. She glanced up from the form up at him, eyes glittering again. Stupid kids, stupid desk duty. "Just—stay here. He won't come in. I'll be back in a minute." She hesitated, but nodded.

He left the desk and went down the hall to the offices, one ear perked for the sound of the door chime. He knocked on the frame of the Lieutenant's door as he entered.

"Got a sec, L.T.?"

The Lieutenant had plenty of gray around his temples and a hard face. His eyes didn't leave his monitor.

"Rodriguez," he said. "Off the desk already?"

"Had a quick policy question. Just wanted to verify our limitations."

The Lieutenant dragged his gaze up from the screen, looking over his glasses at Rodriguez. Then down at the notebook.

"I got a minor out there looking for a restraining order," Rodriguez said.

"Mhm."

"Against another student."

"Mmmm," the Lieutenant took off his glasses and rubbed his eyes. Then replaced them. "Non-violent stalking?"

"Yeah..."

"Witnesses?"

"Just the victim's notes." Rodriguez waved the notebook. "Very thorough, go back a full year. Pretty clear they should be separated."

The Lieutenant sighed.

"It's not your first rodeo, Rodriguez. You know what we can and can't do here. I don't like it anymore than you do, but policy is policy. Only so much we can do..." The computer chimed and the Lieutenant's eyes shot down to it.

Rodriguez waited a few seconds, then cleared his throat. The Lieutenant looked at him again, surprised and perturbed.

"Rodriguez, unless she can prove that the kid did something worse than follow her around..."

"I know, sir." Rodriguez adjusted his belt. "I know. It's just—he followed her here. I'd like permission to—brush him back? Give him a little taste of the road he's on?"

The Lieutenant stared at him for a moment.

"You have to tell him about the order anyway. How you do it is up to you. Don't cross any lines. Kid's dad is a lawyer, give you five to one on that."

"No bet," Rodriguez said, flashing a grim smile. "Thank you, sir."

The Lieutenant waved him out. He found Emmie by the front desk, holding the completed DD11 form.

"Ready to go, officer," she said, her rigid back to the door.

"Thanks." He took it and sat down. The bagel looked rock hard, but he barely noticed. She hadn't missed a comma on the form. Tough kid, maybe she'll take it well.

"Okay, Emmie," he said. "Time for some good news, bad news."

The hope tumbled out of her face.

"Bad news?" she asked.

"The good news is that this restraining order will keep him at least 100 feet away from you outside of school. The bad news is that getting him transferred out of your school takes more than your word against his." He tapped her notebook. "So. If he gets within 100 feet of you outside of school, football games, your house, movies, anything like that, you tell us and he's in big trouble."

"But he can still harass me at school?" she asked. "The school we both go to every single day for eight hours?"

"He can go to school," Rodriguez said. "But he can't touch you or hurt you."

"He can look, though? He can look at me?"

Rodriguez felt hollow. He couldn't say it, couldn't answer. Stupid fucking desk duty.

Emmie glared at him. He cleared his throat.

"And of course," he went on, "if he ever makes an attempt to harm you, you should call 911 immediately."

"Great. So. Basically, you can help once he's raped or murdered me?"

Rodriguez kept his face straight while his stomach boiled.

"I'm going to talk to him today," he growled, calm as he could. "Explain the rules and let him know how bad this will look on his record. Scare him into leaving you alone."

Emmie stared at him for a long moment. He watched her hardening herself.

"Thank you for your time, Officer."

She turned and stalked out of the building.

Rodriguez waited till she reached the door. Emmie looked left, then quickly turned right. Rodrigues leapt up and crossed the foyer in time to catch the door. He slipped out in time to snatch a scrawny kid's upper arm.

"What the hell, man?!"

"Peter Andrews," he said, letting the uniform do most of the talking. "You and I need to talk."

"Let me go! I didn't do anything!"

"C'mon, son."

"My dad's a lawyer!" the kid shouted. Rodriguez smiled down at him.

"I don't care," he said.

He wrenched Peter around toward the door and the kid's bike clattered to the ground. Emmie's head snapped around, jumping like a rabbit. She took in the scene, Rodriguez hoisting most of Peter's weight by the arm.

Then she shook her head. Giving up on him. She knew it wouldn't work, just as well as Rodriguez did.

"Ow!"

Rodriguez loosened his grip on Peter's arm, just enough that he wouldn't break it.

Emmie had grabbed a bike from the rack at the corner of the building. She hopped on and rode off.

• • •

Two days later, Emmie stood alone before her open locker, frozen in thought. Silence in the hallways of Elmwood High School felt strange to her, but beautiful. She wore a light sweater, loose on her slight frame, and her auburn hair trickled down her shoulders. She sighed into the crisp morning. She probably shouldn't be alone, but she wanted to savor the quiet. The peace.

Emmie struggled to focus at home. She had brothers. Younger brothers. They woke like a pack of goblins then tore through the house, screeching. They sucked up most of Emmie and her dad's willpower. Together, they spent their mornings molding the boys into semi-functional human children. Then her dad disappeared to work, chatting up clients all over the state. Exhausting. A family of bits and pieces. This morning, she'd left her father in the trenches with the boys.

Usually, she wouldn't have exposed herself like this, alone in public, but Peter shouldn't have been a problem anymore. She hadn't seen him in two full days. The best two days she'd had in a long time. He was contained. She'd made sure of that.

Her AP Calculus book bumped the locker on its way out, sending the thin gong of sheet metal echoing down the hall. Funny how silence takes an edge when the echoes of a small sound rush back to you. She used to like that kind of thing.

The click of the door handle echoed down the hall. Emmie froze. She didn't look, couldn't make herself look. *He can't be here. He can't.*

The door swung open as she stared into her locker, heart in her throat, knuckles white on the Calculus book. Someone walked in.

It could have been a teacher, a janitor, or the principal. It could have been President Barack Obama or Judy Blume. It could have been anyone in the world.

She knew the footsteps. They made her shiver. She swore at herself for shivering.

She'd known Peter long enough to appreciate how he'd grown into his ears, arms, and legs. His round face had squared out and running track had trimmed his boyish flab into a muscular frame. After a rough start, puberty had given him something to work with. Even the acne scars gave his otherwise unassuming face a roguish charm. Plenty of girls adored him. Just like her, he had friends and plans for college. He had it together.

Somehow, she, of all the girls in town, had caught his eye. "Ensnared his affections," to use his own stupid, conceited phrasing.

Maybe it could have worked between them. He had a brilliant mind and a bright future. She didn't deny that. She just didn't care. She had tried to reciprocate, tried to feel anything at all for the boy who followed her every move. But when she looked him in the eyes she only saw the hunger. Endless. Ravenous hunger. If that was love, she wanted none of it.

He had convinced himself that she'd "come around." He knew this would all work out, that they'd be together forever, someday.

He smirked and waited. And watched her. Hallways. Lunches. Walks home. He even joined her chess club. He was a decent chess player, but he didn't enjoy it. He did it to be near her. She'd tried to ignore him, but she couldn't. His eyes made her skin crawl. So she'd started hiding away. Avoiding what she loved. Peter had sucked the joy out of everything. Senior year evaporated.

In a fair game with even odds, she could have out-maneuvered him. But. Where she wanted a neat row of pawns, she had unsympathetic, jealous friends. Where she should've had a scything bishop, she'd found useless Rodriguez. Her brazen rook? One distracted, absent parent.

Emmie had found someone, finally, who could help her flip the board. She signed in blood.

And yet, here came Peter.

She shivered again, then clenched her fists tight around the book. She glanced up and down the hallway. Empty, of course. Not a teacher in sight. No witnesses. No help.

He grinned from ear to ear and she looked at his eyes. Hunger mixed with satisfaction. He'd known she would be here. Well, why not? He knew her classes, her schedule, her family, and the shrubbery outside her house. Peter probably knew what color bra she had on. Bile burned her throat at the thought.

"Good morning," he said, ambling to a stop and leaning against the lockers.

"What do you want, Peter?"

"Thought you might get here early to study," he said. "I would love to help."

"No."

She glared at him. He smiled back.

"Look, Em, you're the most—"

"I don't care."

Em. No one called her Em. God, she hated him.

"Just give me—"

"No! I don't care."

"Em—"

He reached for her elbow with a cupped hand.

"Touch me and I will report you to the police."

He chortled. She glared.

"Yeah," he said, the grin again. "Officer Rodriguez had me going there. Stayed up all night, reading policies. I get it." He smiled and put his hands up. "You don't wanna see me outside of class, but they can't kick me out of school. Which means I can still help with your Calculus. You can't stop love with paperwork, Em."

Her face flushed. He knew. Of course he did. But still—he shouldn't be here. She'd mad sure of it. He was supposed to be—contained.

Her breath felt shallow as she watched Peter's hunger fan itself. His hand hovered just an inch below her elbow.

"C'mon," he said. "Let's go study for a while."

Her body reacted without her conscious mind's consent. Something very human woke within her. She pulled the hefty calc book back over her shoulder and swung it around in a beautiful arc. Her throat released a screech. His eyes widened in the split second before she caught him across the skull and the smack of the book echoed up and down the hall. He crumpled to the ground, clutching his head.

She hesitated. Then swept down on him, shrieking, pounding him with the book, again and again. He curled into a ball, crying, begging her to stop. Each dull thud of the book made her feel more powerful than the last.

She shrieked even louder, now slamming the spine of the book into his rib cage. She didn't stop until she felt something snap. A rib. He screeched then, like a child, and she stepped back, astounded.

He lay on the floor. Sobbing. She wondered, numbly, if she'd get in trouble for this. Then she laughed, making him twitch. It had happened at school. It was a school problem. They'd give her detention. Detention! In exchange for a broken, wounded, terrified Peter.

Peter's watery eyes looked up at her from between his arms. His body trembled. He said nothing. The hunger had gone and only terror remained. She grinned, brandishing the book at him.

"Never. Get Near Me. Again," she spat, leaning down. Peter flinched at every word. "You have 23 unbroken ribs in your body and I swear to God I will crack every last one of them if I see you again."

He nodded, quick and sharp. It made him wretch and grab at his head. She grinned, then walked away smiling.

115

Freedom. Her mind and limbs thrummed with the power of it.

Then she recalled the agreement. The blood signature.

• • •

After school, Emmie biked to the mansion, passing the police station on her way.

In a small town, whispers carry a long way. Elmwood whispered of vampires. A sisterhood, powerful beyond reckoning. A Queen on an obsidian throne. Stories ranged from cute to horrifying. Blood sacrifices, illnesses cured, daughters gone missing and sons returned home after long estrangements. Housewives had their theories.

The morning she filled out the DD11, Emmie made one another visit. Her backup plan. Her last resort.

It took Emmie months to work up the courage for that visit. Months of research, planning for contingencies. Months of never getting caught alone, of the sickly feeling of his eyes on her skin, of lying awake and praying not to hear a tap on her window in the night.

When Rodriguez told her—well, he'd tried, but she knew what she had to do. She'd biked out to the mansion and signed a deal.

That night, Emmie slept soundly for the first time in months.

The stone walls of the courtyard stood where they had for decades, maybe centuries. She'd half expected them to have disappeared, slinking back into her nightmares where it belonged. Ivy crept over the stones, but didn't touch the massive wooden gate. Small trees pushed their canopies above the wall, and behind their bright growth, the careworn mansion stood proud and aloof. They kept to themselves, well out of town. No visitors.

Emmie leaned her bike against the wall and slung her satchel over the handlebars. A heavy chain hung down beside the gate, brushing the ivy. Emmie stared at it for a long moment. Then she took a deep breath, reached out, and pulled.

The bell tolled.

She waited. Crows cawed from the mansion's trees.

The gate creaked open. Within, a stately garden brimmed with flowers and fruit trees. A straight path cut through to the mansion's broad doorway, which stood open. Emmie exhaled and entered the courtyard. She didn't turn to look at the gate doors, no one would be there. The Queen had opened them and they swept shut behind Emmie.

A hush blanketed the courtyard, such that Emmie could hear the crunch of her sneakers on the path to the mansion. She took timid steps across the threshold and entered.

Gloomy bluish light fell into the grand space from windows high above. Filtered down, she'd guessed, to protect fragile skin. Dark marble columns soared up to brace the balcony running around the second floor. In shadows between the columns, wax figures of shirtless men in dress slacks held idle poses.

Then she caught sight of the Queen and all else fell into the background. A proud marble staircase stretched up from the foyer, climbing to a landing. From there, the Queen gazed down from an obsidian throne. It glinted, even in the low light, just as her cold eyes sparkled.

A serene smile played on her lips, glistening black to match the throne. She wore a light and elegant dress, one long leg escaping the lavender fabric. She bounced it on her other knee. Emmie tried to remember to breathe.

"Welcome back, Emmie," the Queen called down. "I didn't think you'd be so eager to return."

Knowing tones and a sly smile. Emmie clutched her hands together until her knuckles gave a little pop. She bit back the gasp of pain. The Queen's grin widened, showing just a hint of her perfect white teeth.

"You broke our contract," she called up the stairs, glaring at a point three feet over the Queen's head and ignoring her teeth. Her voice quivered, but she firmed it up. "I dealt with Peter myself."

"Did you now?" the Queen seemed delighted. "How?"

"Nevermind how," Emmie said, leaning into her anger. "He'll leave me alone. Forever. And I did it! Not you! You broke your promise. It's a breach of contract."

"Well now," the Queen smiled and leaned back. "That's... an intriguing thought. Maybe we should ask Peter what he thinks?"

She snapped her fingers and they both heard a manly little, "Ow!"

from the courtyard.

Emmie turned, horrified to see Peter in the doorway. A crow harried him to the doorstep, pecking at his arms and head. As he crossed the threshold, it cawed a final time and retreated.

"Come in and join the party, Peter," the Queen said.

Peter looked at her, then at Emmie. He shrugged and limped into the mansion, one arm across his chest. He stopped beside Emmie, head bowed.

Guilt, of all things, boiled up in Emmie's gut.

"Perfect," the Queen said. "Now that we're all here—"

"No." The word surprised Emmie as it fell from her lips. She said it again, louder. "Whatever you want from us, the answer is no. The deal is off."

The Queen smiled.

"We're leaving. Come on, Peter." Emmie turned her back on the throne and put a hand on Peter's chest up near his shoulder. His eyes widened beneath the bruises as he stared at her.

"Move," she whispered. "Idiot."

"If you leave my home, Peter, you will never have her," the Queen called down. "I think you can see that. Stay and you'll be hers, forever."

Emmie tried to soften her face.

"It's not true," she said. He stared at her now, searching her face.

"Isn't it?"

She looked up at him and tried, harder than she ever had, to love him.

"I just—I shouldn't have come here. We can work this out. Together. Outside. *Please.*"

She smiled, but it felt thin and weak. Peter stared at her.

A sudden gust blasted through the entrance hall. The wind whistled through the pillars and lifted Emmie's hair. The cool breeze felt soothing on her skin. Emmie watched the bruises on Peter's face melt back from green and yellow to purple, blue, light blue, then smooth, supple skin. His skin knit against itself to cover over his acne blemishes. He gave a little gasp and clutched his chest, then prodded the rib she'd broken that morning.

"A little favor for you, dear," the Queen said. "Hated to see you suffer."

Peter's mouth hung open as he stared up at the queen. Adoring. Grateful. Emmie saw a flicker of the hunger.

"Peter..."

He stepped forward, past Emmie.

"I'll stay," he said.

"Good boy," the Queen said. She waved a hand and wind filled the halls again. This time it came dry and hot to the skin. It rose to howl all around them, whipping Emmie's hair into a frenzy. Peter's clothes didn't move. He turned to look at her, alive with the hunger, stronger than he'd ever been. The wind passed through him, carrying something away with it.

His face twisted in fear and he lifted an arm, reaching out for Emmie, then let it drop to his side. His face slackened. The hunger faded from his eyes. Peter looked past her for the first time.

"That's all settled then," the Queen said. "Go and rest, Peter, we'll get you dressed properly later."

A sob rose in Emmie's throat as he turned from her. She watched him disappear into the shadows behind the columns.

"Well, that satisfies the terms of our arrangement, Emmie," the Queen said. "Now, if there's nothing—"

The gate bell rang out. The Queen glared down at Emmie, her head tilted to the side.

"Who else did you invite?" the Queen asked.

"This is Officer Rodriguez of the Elmwood Police!" A bold voice trickled in through the courtyard. "Open up!"

Hope sparked in Emmie's chest. *Rodriguez.*

The Queen barked a laugh, slapped the arm of her throne, and stood.

"A law man! Oh what fun!"

The Queen swept down the stairs with wisps of her flowing lavender dress tumbling through the air in her wake. She looked to Emmie like a storm cloud of flower petals rolling down a dark hill. The young woman stood frozen as the Queen brushed past her, dragging the scent of lavender in her wake.

Emmie tore her eyes away to search the shadows. They could still escape. She'd carry Peter out of here on her back if she had to. She crept into the shadows and found him standing still, staring forward, not even blinking. She tugged on his arm, but he didn't move, so she slipped under his arm and put hers around his waist. She saw no other exits, so she pushed Peter toward the front door, a few paces behind the queen.

He groaned, then took a small step. Then another.

The Queen stopped at the edge of the shadows and flicked her wrist. The courtyard gate swept open.

A portly policeman with a crew cut and a stern expression stood outside the gate, one hand on his gun. Seeing the Queen in the mansion's doorway, he straightened up and pushed his sunglasses to the top of his head. He moved forward into the garden, a slight bend in his knees.

"Elmwood Police," the officer called out. "Can you show me your hands ma'am?"

With a lazy flourish, the Queen raised her hands. Emmie nudged Peter forward, creeping up behind the Queen.

"Good afternoon, to you, too," the Queen replied.

"Good afternoon, ma'am. I'm looking for two kids. Saw their bike's out front. One of them is in violation of a restraining order. Have you seen them?"

Emmie opened her mouth to shout—but couldn't. When she tried the scent of lavender came crashing through her mind and her vocal chords contracted. In a panic, Emmie threw Peter off and stepped forward. Rodriguez couldn't see them in the shadows, she needed to get to the light. Two strong hands snapped around her upper arms and held her back. Emmie tried to scream again, but nothing came out. Peter held her tight.

"This building is abandoned," the Queen said, her voice bounding through the courtyard. "No one lives here. You never found the bikes you were looking for. Repeat that back to me."

Officer Rodriguez blinked, then repeated every word.

"Now, go," the Queen said, waving him off. Rodriguez nodded and turned away.

"HELP!" The shriek scorched Emmie's throat as it tore past her constricted vocal chords. "PLEASE, GOD, HELP ME!"

Then the scent of lavender crashed through her skull with such force that she swooned and retched. Peter held her upright. The Queen turned back to look at Emmie, her eyebrows arching high. She was impressed, not concerned. She turned back to the cop.

Officer Rodriguez had turned back to face the mansion. He held his gun in shaking hands and glared at the Queen. He tried to speak, but nothing came out. The Queen cocked her head to the side, then smiled at him.

"Go!" she commanded, voice ringing through the courtyard. Rodriguez holstered his gun, then turned and walked to his squad car. He dropped into the driver's seat. The tires crunched gravel as he pulled away.

Emmie whimpered. Peter held her.

The Queen gave a final, lazy snap of her fingers. The courtyard gates swung shut, then the mansion door.

PAUSE.

A sponsor of the book encourages you to read and interact with the following poem.

Read.

Slowly.

Breathe in on the first line of each couplet.

Pause to consider.

Breathe out on the second line.

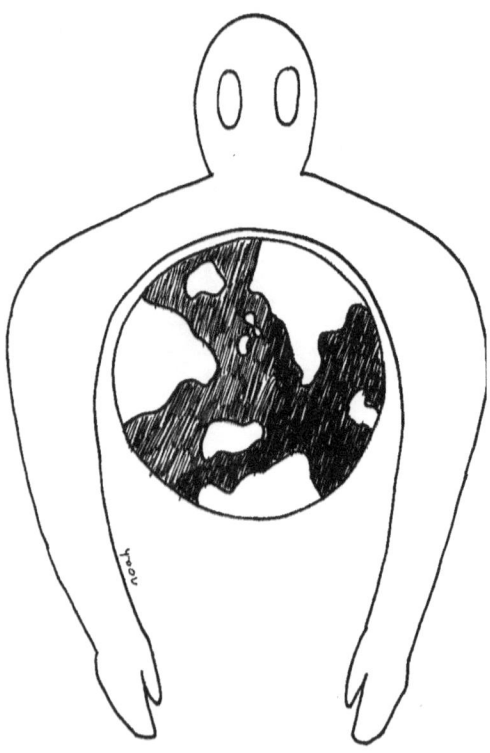

World Breather

written by Daniel Abson and illustrated by Noah Abson

Imagine a world
  where you make all the rules.

Imagine the beings
  that will inhabit your world.

Imagine the civilisations
  that the beings of your world will build.

Now, see how societies rise and fall
  as your world's beings live and die.

Now, enter into your world
  and live as one of those beings.

You will have no memory of its making
  you will have no memory of yourself.

You will love, work, breathe, and die there
  and then you will live, breathe, work, and love there again.

You will be every being in your world
  from its beginning to the end of its time.

Mickey Went

Two sweating bottles of beer clunked down in front of Tom and Clifton on the pock-marked bar. They thanked the bartender in low tones, clinked bottles, and took a slug. Familiar smells: beer, sweat, saltwater, and a hint of dried fish guts; Clifton felt at home, at ease. Fishers, dock workers, and captains of varying shapes and sizes perched on wooden stools. Dusky light trickled through the grime. When a particularly strong swell swept past the pilings below their feet, the dock swayed just a bit. Just enough to let them feel the closeness of the water. As the two men sat, the dock gave a long, gentle pull, letting them know the swell had strengthened after sunset.

"Hol-eeee shit, I think that might be Mickey. Is it?" Clifton asked Tom. The older man nodded his white stubbled chin toward a secluded table in the back of the bar. Tom peered back to find a man in a wheelchair, legs ending at the thigh. He drank alone at the table, but sat high and back in his chair, proud as a pelican. He had a long gash down the side of his face and wore a contented grin. When the dock rolled, his chair wheels did too, but his head stayed still.

"Could be," the younger man replied. "Never knew him, before my time."

"Yeah, well, there's mud minnows out there older than you," Clifton said with a grin. Tom chuckled and rolled his eyes.

"Maybe so. Looks like a decent hand. You ran charters with him or something?"

Clifton chuckled.

"Run charters with him? No. No I never did. But he's something. Something else."

Tom gave him an incredulous look.

"I mean—Mickey," Clifton said. He paused, picking at the label on his beer bottle. "Mickey is Mickey. You ain't heard the stories?"

"I've heard the name and some claims," Tom replied, sipping his beer. "A little too much to believe, if I'm honest. I mean, everybody out here's got stories, sometimes they get—" Tom licked his lip, hesitated.

"What? What about 'em?"

"They get—uhm—embellished," Tom said.

Clifton smirked as he nodded.

"Sure they do. Sure. That ain't the way it was with Mickey though. He's the real deal."

Tom glanced back, watched Mickey roll over another swell.

"Is or was?"

Clifton didn't answer. Flakes from his bottle's label littered the bar top. He picked at it further. Then sipped. Picked again.

Tom's gaze wandered up to the faded 4 x 6's and Poloraoids tacked on the wall above the bar. Dozens of game fish, proud boats, and weathered faces. In their midst, half-buried, was the only sign in the bar, "Free Beer! Tomorrow!"

Tom raised his beer and extended an uncalloused finger toward one of the curling photos.

"That him there?"

Clifton squinted up at the photos.

"Well there's Paul and Michael. There's Peter and John—Jimmy and Daniel. Matt."

"Got the whole New Testament Kickball Team on the wall here, huh? Was Jesus the coach or the pitcher? I meant that one—" he pointed, "the guy on the end of the pier. Stormy."

"Smart asses wake up under the dock—usually with wings or horns..." Clifton said, absently, squinting hard at the photo. "Yeah, that's Mickey."

Mickey stood on the end of a long dock, cast in hues of blue and gray. White caps fretted over the surface and a burst of spray hung suspended above the harbor's stone jetty.

"In his prime," Clifton went on. "I remember that storm actually..."

"Course you do," Tom said. "This one of the first hurricanes after the Ice Age or something?"

Clifton ignored him, gaze locked on the picture. He tipped his bottle back and finished it. Tom signaled the bartender for two more.

"You gotta understand—Mickey was the heart and soul of this dock," Clifton said, bumping his hand on the bar to punctuate his words. "Him and his Palomina. He knew us all by name and boat. Knew what we'd pulled in that week, where we'd been running, who'd helped who and who got snubbed. In fair weather he'd come and go, pull in a few fish on the 'Mina or sub in on a charter. Hung around on the edges of things, cheerful enough, but always one eye on the horizon. "

"Unofficial mayor kinda guy," Tom offered.

"Yeahhh..." Clifton replied, hazy, unsure. "No. No, not like that. More than that. When the sun was out and the fish were running, he was just another captain. Wasn't till things got nasty that you noticed Mickey and the Palomina. Mayor? More like a one-man, volunteer, Coast Guard cutter."

Clifton paused.

"He didn't just know us, you know? He knew her."

He chucked his jaw toward the ocean.

"Knew her like you get to know an old friend. Better than most men know their wives."

Tom sent a sour grunt down into his bottle. Clifton grimaced.

"Sorry. Poor choice of words," he said.

"Nah," Tom said with a dark little smile. "Poor choice of wife."

"Happens," Clifton said, with a nod.

They drank together.

"Like it better here anyway," Tom said. The piling's swayed under their stools. "Air's fresher." He nodded up at the picture. "So the storm—you remember that one?"

"Oh yeah," Clifton squinted. "Yeah. Big one. Real nasty. Flooded this bar up to the tops of the stools, eventually. Wrecked a quarter of the harbor—took a lot from us..."

Tom glanced down at stoolseats, dubious, then up at the picture.

"Doesn't look so bad?"

Clifton gave this a sour grunt.

"Course not! That's from the morning. See the light there? Outta the east? That storm blew in late. We'd seen some nasty ones that year, sure, shutters flapping, roofs peeled up, but nothing near as brutal at that bitch. Swells like houses and 80 knot gusts."

Tom raised his eyebrows. The pilings swayed beneath them. Clifton stared at the picture, beer halfway to his lips, long enough for Tom to start worrying that he'd had a stroke.

He put the bottle down.

"It's always worst when it's rising, 'cause you never know for sure how bad it's gonna get," he said, gesturing to the photo. "Even at dawn, we had some hefty swell in the water and the sky was an ugly yellow going to purple-ish. We'd all felt the power in the water for days, storm's coming for sure. Now, with the sky glowing like a bruised peach in mid-morning, no one's leaving port, right? We spent the morning battening up the houses, hauling out boats and tying them down. After that, what can ya do but sit and wait? So, I was here with a couple old buddies, Donny and Rob, drinking and waiting for her to blow in."

"Ah yeah," Tom said, "Think you've mentioned them before."

Clifton nodded, slow.

"Sure I did, good fellas, good sailors. Not too bright, though. That's them there, two down from Mickey."

Tom found the photo: a pair of sun-tanned, shabbily clad fishermen stood on the dock and beamed down the lens. A weather-worn trawler floated behind them.

Clifton took a long sip.

"He loved that damn boat. Anyway. We're all set up at the bar when a group of fellas comes marching past, laughing." He waved one gnarled hand toward the door, open to the docks. "New visors, rods, poles, coolers. Didn't have a real captain with 'em, just some city-bred assholes with a boat. No offense intended."

Tom grinned.

"Some taken, but go on."

"Fair. So, some—assholes. Idiots. You know what I mean, just didn't give a damn what we told 'em. Gonna run out and pull in a boatload of Albies while we're all sucking our thumbs, then scamper home ahead of the storm."

"Stupid," Tom said.

"Exactly, stupid. We told 'em. But they marched on down the dock anyway."

He was smiling, strutting two fingers down the bar.

"So—what, they went out and Mickey towed them home?"

Clifton wagged a finger at him.

"Nope. Get us another round and I'll tell ya," the old man rose from the stool. "Gotta run the bilge."

He trundled off toward the bathroom, knees wobbling, but head steady through the swells.

Tom finished his beer and realized he had the edge of a buzz already. He ordered two more and glanced back into the shadows. Mickey sat in his chair, apart from the crowds. He finished a beer and set it down. Tom expected him to wheel up to the bar, but another gray-haired fisherman approached Mickey, shook his hand, left a full beer and took away the empty bottle. Mickey smiled, lifting the beer in a small, grateful salute. The man moved away.

Mickey turned suddenly and caught Tom's eye. He winked. Tom looked away quickly.

Clifton huffed and groaned as he eased back onto his stool.

"Where were we?"

"Uhm—some frat boys from down the island were about to get themselves killed," Tom said.

"Ahhh, perfect! They didn't get killed or rescued. Instead, they got the mother of all ass-kickings without leaving the harbor!"

Clifton chuckled, Tom smiled.

"After they'd gone by, we were sitting around joking about it, about how bad it was gonna go for them. Well, someone pointed out that they'd probably get killed. Then someone else said they'd need to get picked up by a real boat, that someone would have to—well, that Mickey would go get them. Save their asses. And then someone—"

He paused, set down his beer and tapped the table with a finger.

"Some wiseass—mighta been me, don't remember—pointed out that we shouldn't have to save them. No sense drowning good men to save idiots. It'd make more sense to just keep them from going out to begin with. Right? Just make sure they don't leave the harbor.

Problem solved. We started agreeing with each other, nice and loud. Few minutes later there's a group of guys heading down the dock. May as well have gone with torches and pitchforks." He barked a phlegmy laugh. "Hah! They dragged those morons off their boat and roughed them up pretty good. Then the cops showed up."

"Oh?"

"Oh yeah," Clifton's smile cracked wider. "This is my favorite part, second favorite maybe. The cops show up, ready to arrest the local drunks, right? We explained the situation to them and they arrested the idiots!"

He cackled to himself and slapped the bar. Tom chuckled along with him.

"On what charge?!" Tom asked.

"Inciting a riot! Hah! A riot, in this tiny little drinking village. Ahhh, shit those were good days."

They laughed together.

"So, Mickey never went out?" Tom asked, nodding toward the photo.

"Oh no, he did," Clifton said. "He did."

He sighed and the smile slid from his face.

"We got back to the bar—a last round before the storm—lots of boasting and playbacks and who hit who with what. Good natured. My buddies, Rob and Donny, were right in the thick of it. Those two—"

He shook his head, smiling down at the bottle.

"Thick as thieves, Rob and Donny. Loved those idiots. Proud and dumb. They started talking... They knew the water, knew the fish. A quick run, no other boats in the way. Rob had that trawler, good size, they figured they could manage the swell."

He coughed a few times.

"I'd been caught out in a mean one the month before—scared me good. They left me. Laughed, grabbed a few more beers, and took off. Engine roaring out of the harbor."

Tom hitched up an eyebrow.

"And the rest of you let 'em go?"

"Oh yeah," Clifton said. "Sure. Can't talk sense into a local. 'Sides, they were out of the harbor in a blink. Nothing much we could do but switch on two radios, one to NOAA for the weather and the other to Channel 13. Wait for the Mayday call."

Clifton subsided, picking at the fresh label on his beer, adding to the pile of flakes.

"So what happened?"

"Ah. Right. Well—It got quiet in here. Spooky; like a wake. The radio would crackle with static and we'd all freeze—but it always went silent again.

NOAA's going on and on about the swell cresting up to 30 plus feet just offshore. We can damn-near feel the waves rolling across the bottoms of the floorboards here in the harbor. Scared me.

Then we heard an engine in the harbor and all ran out."

Clifton let his gaze wander out the door; the grays darkened as the sun went down beyond the storm clouds.

"It was the Palomina. That crazy fool was taking her out into the rising storm. He called into the Harbor Master, just said he'd be back soon. I've never seen a bigger smile than the one on Mickey's face when he left the harbor that day. We could see his pearly whites from the dock. Just a mad grin, and all of us watching the spray bash up 40 feet above the jetty rocks."

A large swell rocked the bar and he paused as it went by. Conversations dimmed throughout the bar, then picked up again as the pilings stilled.

"They disappeared into the swell; Palomina heaving up on those crests the second she left the harbor's mouth. We filed back in and waited as long as we could. Still nothing from the damn radio. Storm's scratching at the door, swell rocking the bar, wind's howling. Howling. Eventually, guys trickled out. Families were waiting. Dogs. They all had their reasons. It got good and dark—the water started clipping up over the dock..."

Clifton had the whole label off his beer. Now he ran a thumb nail over the ridges of adhesive left on the glass.

"The old bartender killed the power. Left me with the radio, a flashlight and a handful of batteries. Nice guy. Then he went home. I stayed and listened. Alone... Felt like if I got up and left that radio—"

Clifton laughed without mirth and shook his head, glancing up at the picture.

"Anyway. I stayed right there. Pretty soon the water came up high enough that waves would send water into the bar. And I—I was worried about it, but the radio seemed more important. Being there seemed important. I sat there in the quiet, listening to the water rise and letting my boots get wet. Waiting. Near as stupid as Donny and Rob going out in the first place..."

Clifton glanced down at his legs, then over to Mickey, briefly.

"When the radio crackled again, it scared me so much I fell off my damn stool into the water." A crooked smile leapt to his face. "Freezing cold. Sobered me up pretty good. When I came up, Mickey was on the radio. Said he had two fellas on board and was making for port."

Clifton shook his head.

"Man was a miracle of miracles. I took the flashlight out to the docks and waved it around overhead, probably looked like a drunk little lighthouse. The harbor was a damned mess; boats everywhere, decking floating around. Had my arm hooked around a piling as the waves slammed past, but I wasn't going in till they made it. Wood was creaking like it could give any second."

The old man laughed, chin bristles waggling like a pad of tiny antennae.

"Stupid. Stupid thing to do. Clinging there for my life when I could have been up on shore... Anyway, it didn't take long—Mickey came puttering past in the Palomina and I helped him find a nice calm spot in the shallows. Then I helped him unload—"

Clifton stopped hard, swallowed, then went on.

"Well—come to find out that the trawler capsized. Mickey found the boat, a miracle in itself, and Donny had a line wrapped around his arm, clinging to the hull. Mickey had to dive in and drag him back to the 'Mina. Middle of a storm like that—crazy. Shouldn't have worked. Humans ain't built to survive water like that—and they got back to the boat. Doesn't make sense... Never made any sense..."

Clifton stopped again, shaking his head.

"And Rob?" Tom asked.

Clifton shook his head, eyes tight.

"The other fella was a stranger," Clifton said, down to his empty bottle. "Some adventurous-type sailing up to Maine from the islands. Solo. Got caught in it and capsized not far from the boys."

"Wait so, Rob—?"

"Never found him."

"Shit," Tom said. "I'm sorry, Clif. That's—tough."

Clifton sniffed in a breath and nodded.

"Yeah. Well. It happens. Can't save 'em all, I guess. I left for the islands that winter. Didn't come back for a long time."

They sat there together, watching the storm breeze ruffle the edges of all the photos along the bar.

"Lot of missing faces when I got back," Clifton said. "Mickey's was one of them."

"Where'd he go?"

Clifton shrugged.

"Asked around, no one seemed to know," Clifton said.

"And his legs?"

Clifton shrugged.

"Same thing," Clifton said. "Don't know. Seems like—"

"Seems like what?" Tom said. "His legs are missing."

Clifton nodded.

"Of course, just that, well, he did things; things that no man—no mortal man could have done."

Clifton's eyes stayed locked on his bottle. Tom's eyes narrowed, then his cheeks puffed out in a big exhale.

"What are you trying to say?"

Clifton's brows drew down, tugging the leathery wrinkles together around his eyes.

"Just that—nothing's free, is all. Nothing's free. Mickey was good to us. Too good, maybe, for too long."

Tom reflected on this and tapped his beer bottle.

"Well, I mean—you could go ask him, right?" Tom said. "Why don't you go talk to him?"

But Clifton had frozen again, staring past the photos above the bar.

Tom finished his beer.

"Clif?"

"Yeah?"

"I asked if you were gonna—"

"Go talk to him. Yeah, I heard ya," Clifton replied.

The old man waved a gnarled hand at the bartender, then produced a handful of crumpled cash from a jacket pocket and smoothed it out on the bar. The bartender glanced at the pile briefly.

"Extra one for Mickey?"

Clifton nodded. Beers slid up and down the bar. Clifton turned to face the back corner of the bar. Mickey smiled at him and raised his beer. The old man returned the gesture. They took a slug together.

Tom watched, brows knit.

"What? That's it? That's all? Was that a conversation?" he asked.

"Something like that," Clifton said with a small smile. He turned back to the bar and let his gaze drift over the photos. "Something like that."

Mickey Went

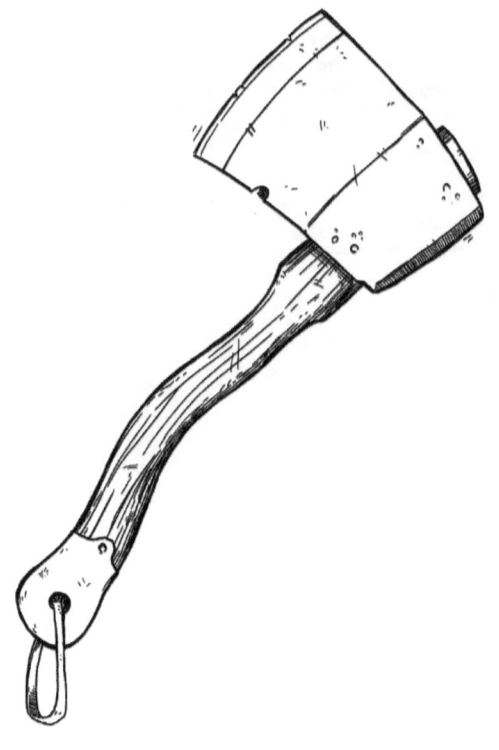

The Sheriff

Sporadic musket fire shook tree trunks deep in the woods of Massachussets. The *cracks* and *pops* died off, replaced by the *thud* and *thunk* of hatchets, the *shick* and *snick* of bayonets.

In just a few blinks it ended. The stillness of the forest prevailed.

Bodies lay still or gave final twitches as souls leaked from veins to soil. Brown clad and red, every unmoving uniform bore tears and dark blooms. The living, all in brown, moved among the bodies, pulling free boots, gold teeth, ammunition—slitting throats where appropriate. They tread softly and did not speak.

Lionel had survived. Lionel always survived. He stood over the Red Coat he had killed with his hatchet. He'd parried a bayonet thrust, grabbed the hot musket barrel, pulled the Redcoat close, then hewn his neck at the shoulder. Arterial blood had spouted up and out, coating Lionel's face with warm splatter. He tasted otherness of the man's life force.

Breath hissed through his clenched teeth as the Redcoat slumped to the ground before him. The ringing in his ears faded slowly in the quiet woods. His heart slowed. He spat to clear his mouth of blood.

He knelt by the corpse, gently shutting the man's eyes. Then cut off a clean patch of the white undershirt. Lionel doused it in water and scrubbed the gore from his face and neck. Not much he could do for his clothing except hope to find a stream before he began to reek.

He froze with the cloth on his cheek. A cabin nestled into the woods just across the clearing. Hidden. One room, log built, stone chimney. Innocent and tucked away from the war on this backwoods trail.

Other militiamen had noticed it as well. Finding him hale and prepared, the sergeant nodded to Lionel. He nodded back, reloading his musket.

They stalked toward the cabin together, Lionel in front. The rest of their force remained in the clearing. Lionel announced himself as a soldier of the American Militia. He asked to see their hands in the air.

Blood still drying on his tunic, Lionel stepped across the threshold of the cabin. A woman stood with her hand on the shoulder of a young boy. Though freshly laundered, her plain dress and his too-small shirt bore old stains.

String-tied clusters of dried herbs and flowers hung from every rafter. On the table, a book lay open to a page titled: *Potente healers of hex-borne maladies.* Lionel knew to expect the crisp illustration of St. John's Wort—knew the next page detailed a recipe for a tincture. He looked back up to the herbs. *Meadowsweet, Poppy... St. John's Wort.*

A breeze shifted in the clearing, slipped through the open kitchen window, tickled the mortar and pestle, and drifted to the militiamen.

The herbaceous scent made Lionel blink.

He saw the kitchen of his childhood home, a crisp spring day, bright light on his mother's smile. She hummed while she ground down dried herbs for a fresh tincture.

He blinked the image away.

The kitchen again, this time the dark. He didn't want to see, didn't want to look down, but he did. His mother, face down, her hand cold in his warm fingers. No blood. No wounds. Stone dead.

Herblore. Witchcraft.

Lionel blinked again and sniffed in a quick breath, the cords of his neck tightened as he fought to land in the present. In the small cabin in the woods, surrounded by herbs. A witch. A boy.

The woman spoke, professing their simple, steadfast neutrality. Do no harm. They had a rifle for hunting, an ax for wood, and a slingshot for small game. They simply lived.

Lionel breathed, steadied himself.

The mother clutched her child close with one hand as he clung to her skirts. The other she held behind her. She waited.

Lionel raised his musket. The sergeant called for him to stand down. Lionel did not. The witch kept a hand behind her back. She did not scream, did not even blink.

"Lionel, stop this at once!" the sergeant shouted. Lionel ignored him.

"What's your name, boy?"

"Ernest," the boy whispered. *Strong, confident, proud.*

"I need to talk to your mother alone, Ernest," he said. "Go wait outside."

He looked up to his mother. Slowly, one arm behind her still, she leaned down to kiss him on the forehead.

"Go on," she said. "I love you."

He hesitated—but nodded and moved toward the door. Lionel and the witch stared at one another. Light filled the cabin as he opened the door, then dimmed again as it shut behind him.

"You hereby stand accused of witchcra—"

A twitch of her hips, swirling skirts, the barrel of a rifle appeared. She raised it. Lionel fell to his right, firing. Her muzzle flashed and two roars rattled the cabin. An angry buzz whipped past Lionel's ear as he fell. The witch spun and fell to the dirt in a heap of skirts.

Lionel leapt up and drew his hatchet. She didn't stir.

A wet sound and a whimper came from behind him. He turned to find the sergeant, crumpling to his knees, both hands to his throat. Blood poured through the man's fingers, darkening the chest of his uniform. His torso thudded to the floor beside the witch.

Breath hissed through Lionel's teeth. He eased his hatchet free. Window light flashed on its silver edge as he approached the witch.

· · ·

Flames from the cabin's roof reached up to blacken the bows of the towering maples. Green leaves curled into twisted knots of char.

Miles away, Lionel crept through the woods with the boy on his back. The tiny head on his shoulder shuddered at odd intervals and left a small, warm patch of damp on his shoulder.

Lionel spoke to the boy of the wickedness of witches and the glory of the young republic for which they fought. Paradise on Earth.

Becoming Prey

I'd misjudged a few things. I see that, in hindsight.

Actually, I saw it pretty well at the time, too.

When you plan an illegal salvage dive to Old Charleston, you plan to *not* bump into the Allegiance Navy while you're there. And yet.

"Stay still, Lem," I told Lemming, who floated beside me, still as the staghorn coral sprouting from the fireplace behind him.

"Aye, Sarge," he replied in a soft voice. "Thought we'd be alone for this one."

Four years out of the service and Lem still followed me around like a good-natured remora.

"We were led to believe that..." I replied, watching the orange dive suits paddle through the drowned and dilapidated city below us. It looked like an entire division, a hundred sailors, at least. "But *why* are they all here?"

"Salvage, maybe? Same as us?" Lemming suggested.

"Naval divers on salvage... Could be that, Lem," I said. "Could just be that."

"Sorry, Sarge. But. Well then, what *are* they doing here?"

"I think," I replied slowly, "that it doesn't matter. Let them kick on by—then we get to work on that vault."

"Of course, Sarge. Wait 'em out and work quick."

So, we lurked in the townhome and I assessed the formation out of stubborn, old habit. Their squads were loose and their pace was all wrong. They'd flash headlamps through doorways and move on. Too fast to call it a thorough search, but too slow for a routine patrol. Must have been a real dry-behind-the-ears lieutenant in command. Based on what I could see, I'd have bet even their laser pistols and mechgills were under-charged.

Like ours, their dive suits covered them from toe to tip. Unlike ours, each one had a bulge on their back where the slits of their mechgills could pull air from the water. Lem and I sported a pair of old hyper-compression flasks. They weigh less and run quieter, but they put us on the clock.

The soldiers' long flippers lifted clouds of silt behind them, even from a few feet off the old cobblestone road. New lieutenants fear the open blue. They feel safer hiding in the old streets, shadowed by the ruins. I'd have kept that division a good twenty feet off the floor, entering buildings through roofs and windows, with threats of hard labor to punish any squad leader dipping too low and kicking up mud.

They brought a lot of hardware for this little excursion...

"Lem, can you get their comms for us?"

"Let me see..."

The Allegiance Navy talked a big game and had a track record to back it up. With ninety-five percent of Earth under the sea, the nations with the biggest, baddest fleet of boats and submarines tend to carry the most clout. Well. On the surface they did.

Down here, though... down here, power is fickle. If you feel safe, you're probably about to die.

Lem snorted.

"Should have been a challenge," he said, "but their C.O. has them on an unsecure channel."

"Sloppy. Pipe 'em in. Make sure it's one-way."

"Sir."

Another pause, then a tinny overture of radio chatter leaked into my headset.

— *Palomino to Mustang, finished in Delta sector and moving to Echo.*

— *Confirmed, Palomino, move to Echo sector.*

— *Clydesdale to Mustang, nothing in Juliette, moving north.*

— *Confirmed, Clydesdale.*

— *Roan to Mustang, we just covered Echo sector. Moving to Golf.*

A sharp pain pinned my eye to its socket. *Asinine. Idiotic. Dangerously disorganized.*

— *Mustang to—*

— *Palomino to Mustang, please confirm move to Echo sector.*

— *Negative, Palomino. Move to Hotel. Roan, confirming your move to Golf.*

I found my teeth ached from clenching and I had to focus on relaxing my jaw. The grating of this commander's self-assurance against his ineptitude—and we were stuck waiting on it to clear. The whole situation made me want to slice his air hose.

— *Roan copies, Roan out.*

— *And Mustang to all squads, keep your focus on the search. I want the objective in hand and our feet dry in no more than thirty-five minutes. We don't want the next division stealing our glory.*

— *Mustang, out.*

I waved a hand in front of Lem and made a cutting motion. I needed to think. *And if I have to listen to that mudfish give another stupid order...*

Thirty-five minutes. That would give them about fifteen more minutes of searching before they had to start the ascent. Too fast and too slow. And still no real clues as to why they were here.

Comprehension niggled at the back of my mind. The voice and the squad names had jostled my memory without shaking the details loose. *Foreign accent. Extinct species.*

"I know that voice," I said. " 'Mustang.' Why do I know that voice?"

"Nigel, sir. You trained him. Loved 'the ponies,' as he called them."

I think I'd called him "an unteachable slob" and "an eighty kilogram anchor tied to the balls of society" at various points in his training. Someone gave him a sergeant's stripe before I left the service. Probably not that long before I left, come to think of it. I doubt he'd be happy to find me here.

"What did you boys call him, 'good-for-nothing Nigel'?"

"'Good-for-nought.' He had some of his family's old British accent."

"Good-for-nought. Clever."

"Not particularly, sir. It must be true what they say about failing up."

"Mm. You recognize *Roan* or *Palomino's* voices?"

"No, sir, but they sound nervous."

"You would be, too, with that idiot leading your dive."

"Too right, sir."

"Mm. So. What does this mean for us?"

"Well, sir," Lem replied. "We can assume that Nigel will be Nigel."

"Lucky us," I replied, watching the flippers disappear and wondering how many of those men would be dead by the end of the year. People see an orange suit and they feel the almighty power of the Allegiance Navy. Really, it's just a thin layer of neoprene stretched over a frightened kid who needed a free meal. And eventually the lanky bastard will find themself at the wrong end of a laser pistol—or the flagrant stupidity of their commanding officer.

"Sir?"

"What's that, Lem?" I said.

"Should we head on? While they're blinded by the mud?"

The mud clouds had thickened into a boiling soup. We could only catch flashes of orange amongst the murky brown now. They were blind. It gave me a horrible crawling sensation, followed by a spark of optimism.

"Almost," I said. "We'll move before that next division gets down here. Use the silt for cover."

"Yes, sir. Gonna be tight on air," Lem said, helpfully.

I glanced down at my wrist and cursed. Fifty-six minutes left on the tank. Our informant had given us a large radius of downtown Old Charletson to search and the description: stone walls, topped by monkey gargoyles. It had taken us hours to find it. And just when we did... Lem had caught that flash of orange up the street. We'd dipped out of sight, hunkering down in the skeletal remains of a townhome. Seawater and coral growth had eaten through the soft furniture and trimmings. You could still get a sense for the kind of comfort these assholes had enjoyed, though. Made me sick with jealousy. Lem and I glared up at those gargoyles lining the stone wall across the street, breathing too much of our air.

We still had to navigate through the house, find the old hydro vault, get a microbubble on the door, drill the door, drybag their precious documents, and get back to the ship. Oh, and decompress. An hour's work, if it all went well.

"You're not wrong, Lem," I muttered. "But we do pretty well in a tight spot."

"Typically, Sarge, typically we do. Comes from being in so many tight spots, I'd expect."

I gave him a grunt. We waited. The gargoyles lurked.

"Alright, Lemmy," I checked my watch, fifty-three minutes of air left. "Up and over. Heading two-two-three, not a hair off or we'll be sleeping in the nearest Naval Detention Center."

"Aye, sir," Lem said, quietly. Not frightened, not nearly frightened enough.

I pushed back from the window, crossing the worm-ridden flooring to get to the staircase. Something shot up out of the floorboards with a flash of bubbles and bluish gray skin. I fired. The bright white lance of light took it through the center and burned a hole through the wall behind it. I felt the sudden heat in the water even through the thick skin of my suit.

A crab the size of my chest floated back down to the desiccated floorboards, a neat hole through its broad shell. Dinner for the other bottom feeders.

I looked up through the tiny hole in the wall, no orange suits that way. Slowly, I turned around and looked back out of the front window. A squadron slipped away around the corner, leaving a cloud of brown muck behind them. I exhaled and glanced at Lem. He stared down at his tablet and had his face pinched in concentration.

I waited.

And waited.

Finally, he shrugged and tapped the tablet.

"Clear, Sarge," he said. "They're still on the move. Nice shot."

"Lucky," I said.

"Not for the crab, sir." He grinned.

"I meant lucky they didn't—" I sighed. "Yes, Lem; shit day to be a crab. Let's head on. Calmly."

"Yessir. Right behind you."

I ascended the stairwell with slow, deliberate kicks. I kept my pistol out, but reminded myself to identify objects before putting holes in them. Nigel had his squads on edge. Jumpy. Any rogue laser fire near them and he'd probably have them boil the ocean returning fire.

It occurred to me, briefly, that we could swim right off this job. Just give it up — hand *Annie's Revenge* over to the next repo boat that pulled up, get back in the Navy, training lieutenants, fighting to keep the Nigels of the world behind clipboards where they belonged. I'd get a little apartment in New Denver or Fort Collins. Some where I could look out at the water. Relax. Get old.

"Okay there, Sarge?" Lem asked.

"What? Yeah, why?"

"It's just—you were swearing to yourself. Again. A lot."

"Oh. Yeah. I'm fine. We're fine, Lem," I said, before clamping my mouth.

He didn't reply.

The staircase rose two floors up until we had nestled among the rafters and could stare out at the great ocean blue stretching away forever. I shivered at the largeness of it. Weak sunlight wobbled down to the pockmarked remains of the rafters. I poked my head over the lip of the front wall.

Clouds of silt rose between the buildings now. It looked like the gooey brown soul of the dead city making a last, awkward reach for sunlight.

Nigel's squads had all moved west and I couldn't make out any signs of the next division diving in from the east.

"Moving out," I said. Squeezing between two rafters, I rose above the building.

Something grabbed one of my flippers. I spun and took aim without hesitating and had a couple pounds of pressure on the trigger before I recognized Lem.

"What?!" I shouted, quickly pulling the pistol out of his face. He never flinched. Damn him, he never flinched.

"Sorry, sir!" Lem said. He gazed, serene and curious, past me and out into the blue beyond. Sunlight glinted in his eyes, then a dark shadow covered us both. Something about it prickled the hair on my neck. He let go of my flipper and pointed up. My gaze snapped around and I... gurgled.

"My thoughts exactly, sir," Lem replied.

The word "shark" doesn't capture the scope of the thing. It could have swallowed *Annie's Revenge* in a go. It eclipsed the sun for several moments as it continued a slow loop down toward the submerged rooftops. My mouth ran dry watching its tail sweep back and forth in massive, lazy strokes. Completely silent and completely at ease. I felt the sudden smallness of my form, the fragility. I found myself making the prayer of those preyed upon: *Please, great powers above or below, let that monstrosity pass without noticing me.*

"You ever seen one that big, Sarge?" Lem whispered.

I tried to respond but the fear held my chest too tight. The "shark" drew lower and swam around the pitted frame of a church steeple. For an insane moment, I pictured it smoking that steeple as I would smoke a tapered cigar.

"No, never," I choked out. "Is there a name for it?"

"'Shark', sir? Maybe 'Megalodon'?"

I ground my teeth and glanced down. No one swam for cover. No one reacted. The silt cloud thickened. *They have to have that on radar. They have to...* The horror in my chest turned outward, toward those squads in the street. Exposed. *Nigel. Nigel's cutting corners to save time. They don't see it.*

"Patch me through to Nigel," I said.

"Sir?"

"Now, Lem."

"Sir."

He tapped a few keys. Gave me an okay sign with his hand. I hesitated, considering whether or not I should impersonate one of his squad leaders. *They're confused enough already.*

Which meant I had to do a dumb thing for the right reasons. My jaw ached as I eased it open to speak.

"Citizen Diver to Mustang," I said. "Come in, Mustang."

My breath sounded loud in my helmet while I waited for an answer.

"Mustang to Diver, this is a Alliance Operation and you're on a secure—you're on an unauthorized channel. Remain where you are."

Lem waved at me frantically between taps of his tablet, pointed down. A squad has detached and paddled toward our building. Exposed out in the wide street.

"Nigel, check your radar."

A long pause while I listened to my breath and the squad reached the middle of the street, laser pistols drawn and aimed at the windows of the building. None looked up. Bad training.

"*Sergeant?!* Are you—are you on a salvage job?! During an active Naval Operation?! Do you have—?"

"Nigel! The radar!"

Someone else cut in on their side of the line, "Sir, we—"

"Not now, Simons!" Nigel spat. To me, he shouted, "This is a Top Secret dive, Sergeant. They'll *hang* you for this, you meddlesome ass!"

The divers had reached our building. Any second now, one will look up...

"Check your flood-damned *radar*, Nigel! You cod-brained... fool..."

The dim street fell to darkness and my words died on my tongue. A gargantuan mass of blue-gray skin swept down into the street. The tips of its pectorals skimmed the wall. The eye passed our building, tall as the windows, black as the depths. It moved in lazy, unconcerned sweeps.

Lem shouted on the Navy's channel, screaming for them to take cover. Too late.

The eye rolled back, the tail flashed; it attacked.

Screams filled my helmet on the Alliance channel, then cut off. It slapped our building, shuddering its studs and bowling us over in a cloud of mud. Lem and I rose just to the top of the cloud.

The sea was empty again. I spun, searching. The shark had disappeared. Pandemonium on the Alliance radio. Flashes of orange kicking up more and more silt in the streets below us.

"Lem?" I whispered.

"Sir?"

My eyes nearly rolled in my head as I probed the inky depths for miles in every direction. Every shadow looked like a leviathan. None were. Were they? My heart pounded.

"Where did it go, Lem?"

"Probably back out to sea, sir," he suggested, voice steady. "Maybe it didn't like the flavor of Alliance."

"Right," I said, turning back to the brown cloud over Charleston. "Right. Let's just get back—"

A gray blast of motion whipped by me, then the shark's tail disappeared into the cloud of silt. Downward. Toward the divers. The power of its tail stroke tumbled me backward over the roof of the townhomes. I recovered with a string of curses and saw Lem frozen, tablet in hand. I swam up and shook him. When he turned to me his face had drained of color. He had to slap the tablet three times before we reconnected.

"They're dying, sir!" he shouted. "By the dozen! We have to—"

"We have to get the hell out of here while that thing is distracted, Corporal!" I shouted, turning to run for it. With a slap of my fins I took off, pumping buoyancy into my suit and kicking furiously toward *Annie*. My breath came in panicked heaves, Lem yelled something, but I couldn't hear it. My heart pounded like a mullet on the dock.

Like a mullet.

Fast.

Too fast.

Conserve air. Decompress.

I checked my watch and saw that I'd hit the first decompression checkpoint already. And I'd burned through half my air. Swearing beautifully, I sucked stale air from my buoyancy vest and hovered there, halfway home. The silence of the blue crushed in on me from miles all around. It's always so much worse when you're alone.

Alone.

"Lem?!" I shouted. a

No response. Static.

"Oh for— ARGH! Poseidon's bristly ballsack! LEM WHERE THE HELL ARE YOU?!"

I searched the distant rooftops. The shark rolled around in the streets of Charleston. Red tinges had started to infect the brown clouds of silt.

My breaths came sharp and loud, painful. *Come on, Lemmm. Come on come on comeoncomeoncomeon Where the wet devil—?*

A flash. A flicker.

A tiny figure drifted above the townhomes. High beams on, firing laser after laser into the roiling brown mess below. Slow, steady rhythm, letting the water cool between rounds. A good soldier.

"You idiot!" I shouted.

Then I froze.

I almost left him. Almost.

Instead I sucked air out of my suit and kicked hard, diving. My head stung. Those seconds felt like hours and the water felt thicker somehow, like it tried to hold me back. I kicked harder, watching.

Lem had a roof beam clamped between his legs. He calmly poured lasers down into the mud. It rose higher and higher, threatening to engulf him too. Flashes of orange and gray showed in the frenzy. Then the cloud exploded. The shark charged Lem. My heart stopped. The *size* of the damn thing—it looked like a battleship bearing down on a mollusk.

Still though. It was just a shark. Maybe I could communicate with it. My laser pistol came up and I fired right over Lem's helmet.

One to the nose, it flinched away to the right. The shot left a scorch mark, but didn't break the skin. I didn't worry about that. Next shot to the gills, the shark flinched back. One more to the eye. It swam off in a circle, the blast of its tail spun Lem up out of the townhome. I felt the water warming around me, I was firing too fast. I needed time to cool off.

The shark came back around in a snap of motion. Lem blocked my aim for a precious second before sailing behind me.

Gills, *flinch*. Nose, *flinch*. Eye, *flinch*.

It kept coming. The water warmed. *Oh. This is gonna hurt,* I thought.

Gills—Nose—Eye. *flinch—flinch—flinch* The heat crinkled my suit. The shark gave a twist of rage. Turned as if to leave. My heart soared.

Then it turned back and shot toward us. Resignation swept through my veins, bracing me.

Gills-Nose-Eye. *flinch-flinch-flinch*

I felt the first trickle of pain. I grimaced, but held my aim, kept firing.

GillsNoseEye. *flinchflinchflinch*

Blossoms of white spread up my arms and across my chest. The heat seared me.

"GILLS, NOSE, EYE YOU BIG STUPID F— ARRRRGGHHHH!!"

Plasma boil. Blinding pain scorched my arms and chest. A fit of bubbles surrounded me. My pistol fell from my cringing hands. I screamed, kicking back. The burn dug down to my nerves in an instant. I whited out and the world went dark.

• • •

I live in *Annie* the way a conch lives in its shell. I know every centimeter of her. We had a ding in the cargo bay's fifth beam, from a transport job a few years back. I lay beneath that dent. I tried to sit up, but couldn't, so I raised my neck to find about a thousand tons of metal on my chest. My torso and arms felt cool and itchy.

I groaned.

"Morning, Sarge," Lem said. I heard two clanking footsteps and his face appeared above me, beaming.

"What the *hell* is this, Lem?" I demanded. Still grinning, he moved away checking one of his nearby screens.

"Nanobot vest, sir," Lem said. "Patching you up."

"Nano—? Lem I *expressly* forbid you to get these. Do you remember that?"

"Yes, sir."

"So what the *hell* is this thing doing on my chest?"

"Patching you up, sir."

"Right, well…" I started. "Right. Let's make sure we find somewhere out of the way to store it."

"Right, sir. Thank you, sir."

"Lem—" My brain got hung up for a moment, unsure which question mattered most. Lem knew, of course.

"The Navy took heavy losses and pulled the orange boys out. The shark followed them back to the ship and got scared off by the long guns. It's still out there."

I grunted.

"But so are we," I said.

"Yes, sir."

I could hear the self-satisfied grin on his face. "Best to rest, sir. We can take another look tomorrow."

I grunted again, then closed my eyes and lay still, trying to ignore the itch.

Pants Half Full

Hank pushed open the door to the bar. A wave of small sounds and large smells rolled out past him. He took a lanky step over the threshold, trying to ignore the squish of the carpet beneath his boots. His nicest pair of boots. Silly to wear them out to this shithole, to catch-up with this lazy sack of fatty tissue. Hank caught a hint of motion, a pudgy hand waved him down from a table in the middle of the bar. Bart held up an empty beer bottle, pointed to it and held up two fingers.

"Next round's on me, I guess," Hank murmured good naturedly.

He bought the beers and sat down across from Bart. They chatted for a while, friends from driving school catching up after a couple years in their rigs. Endless construction on I-20, broken axles and blown tires, cold fronts, storm fronts, all the usual road warrior bull.

Bart seemed a bit jumpy, like he had something to spill, but needed the right moment. Hank did his best to ignore it. He laid out a yarn about a time when he'd counted on a rest station at four in the morning and found it closed. How he'd surprised himself with a tiny squeaker of a fart that turned into a seat full of crap. Bart cackled pretty hard at that one and Hank chuckled along with him.

"Oh yeah," Hank giggled, stretching his long legs and crossing one boot over the other, careful not to scratch them. "Had to pull over and sort myself out. Cab reeked of chili dog runoff. Used up a whole box of wet wipes. Probably wear a damn diaper next time I make that run..." He trailed off, smiling. Then asked, "How 'bout you, Bart, you shit your pants on the road, yet?"

Bart didn't respond for a moment, the levity had fallen from his face and his eyes had gone out in the distance. He faced the door of the bar, but seemed to stare past it.

"Bart?"

Bart shook himself. He looked at Hank across the wobbly table, then down at his mostly empty beer.

"Aw what the hell, ain't like you're gonna believe me anyway," he muttered, half to himself.

Hank's brow furrowed.

" 'Course I'll believe ya. I mean we've all done it," he chuckled.

"Nothing to be ashamed of. We're all just big smelly animals. Sacks of water turning food into crap."

Bart grinned at that, but it felt cold to Hank. Too forced. The big man nodded and leaned forward.

"A'right, Hank," he said, "A'right. So picture... different bar, but same—" He looked around. "Everything. Shitty ol' carpet. Shitty ol' tables and chairs."

"Of course," Hank said. "Your kind of joint." He didn't mean it as a compliment, but the thick man just nodded and plowed on.

"Friday, early afternoon, still a thin crowd, like this, but good energy in the place. Not too dark. I grabbed a beer from the bartender and sat at a table by myself. Waited on a friend to show up. Jeb, outta Saratoga, you know Jeb?"

"Don't think so. You don't mean the Jeb that drives the bright purple piece of shit?" asked Hank.

"Nahhhh, nah. Drives a big red Mac, one with chrome vampire teeth on the grill?"

Hank shook his head, "Never met him." Bart shrugged, finishing his beer and pushing it to the side.

"Doesn't matter. Anyways, I was sitting there waitin' on Jeb, wonderin' how late he'd be. Fifteen minutes go by; I was 'bout halfway through that first cold one when the door creaks open behind me, okay? I raised my bottle for a swig as I turnt to look, thinking it might be Jeb. And I saw—" He shook his head and steeled himself with a puffy exhale. "Hank, I saw myself walk into the bar."

Bart paused. Hank felt his eyes narrow.

"You what?"

"Don't gimme that look, yet—lemme finish," Bart said, brandishing a short, fat finger under Hank's nose. "Knew you wouldn't believe me."

Hank nodded and leaned back in his chair, coaching his face back to normalcy. The lanky man let one hand drift up to touch the reassuring lump in his chest pocket. Bart gave his head tiny shakes, jiggling his loose jowls as he did so. It reminded Hank of a bulldog, but one on the edge of a nervous breakdown. Gutless and close to bolting. His mind drifted back to the old days, when he first got behind the wheel, how the world seemed to widen and grow stranger every time he pulled onto the highway.

"You're right," Hank said, "Driving—it's a strange way to make a living. Been a long time since I thought about it."

Bart ignored him, eyes darting from the tabletop to the door and back. Hank didn't want him to run out, so he sifted through his memories for a story. Not just any story. A strange one. He grinned as it came to him.

"You know once— this was a few years back, now—but I once saw a man with a minivan full of pigeons."

Bart's eyes started to swim back toward the present.

"Pigeons?"

"Yep, pigeons. In a Walmart parking lot. Florida panhandle. Had 'em clutched up in this big silver net."

Bart's eyes narrowed.

"And you know what? He *traded it*."

"Traded the pigeons?"

"Traded the van. With the pigeons in it."

"What?"

"I shit you not. Swapped it for a Ford Escape with a crate of baby alligators in the back."

Bart's eyes narrowed to slits.

"Alligators? You're making this shit up."

"Couldn't if I tried," Hank said, leaning back and smiling. "I ain't the creative type."

"Well, how'd they switch 'em?" Bart asked.

"Didn't," Hank said, with a grin. "They opened their back hatches, showed off their wares, then they swapped keys and drove each other's cars away."

Bart shook his head.

"World's a strange place," he said.

"Exactly. It's a strange place where strange things happen. What I'm trying to say is, I'll give you a fair shake, promise. No more faces."

Hank put a hand to his chest and tried to look solemn. Bart slaked a bead of sweat from his head and shook it off for the carpet to swallow. Then he pursed his lips.

"Hell," he said, wobbling the table as he set the bottle down. "Where was I?"

"You saw you walk into the bar," Hank said, "No pills?"

"No, no, no," Bart said, with a hard shake of this head. He held up a finger. "First beer. Maybe half of one. No uppers, no downers. Dead sober, and I watched me walk into the bar. 'Cept—" he tapped the table with a finger, "I had this uniform on, right? Gray coveralls, but formal. Like a tailored suit, but a full body suit. *Sharp*. Very sharp. Like a Star Trek outfit, kinda. You know Star Trek?"

Hank nodded.

"So, he walked in, looking real outta place in that uniform, and he kind of tip-toed over to my table, like he wasn't supposed to be there, and sat down without a word. He was trimmer than me and older, with a scar across one cheek. I started to ask what the hell he's playing at, but before I can speak he holds up a hand.

" 'I shouldn't be here,' he said, 'and what I'm *not* about to tell you will have dire ramifications.' "

I know, Hank. I know. That's what he said, 'dire ramifications', all dramatic and shit. So I gave him a dirty look and said,

" 'I'm about to ramification one of these beer bottles through your earhole unless you start talking sense.' "

Hank snorted, Bart half-smiled back.

"But he just, well, grinned at me. Not pretty. Kind of crazy. Like he'd like to see me try. Then he shook me up. He said—uhm—

" 'No you won't' he said. All calm and cool. He said, 'Go on and talk bad, but you ain't harmed a soul in twenty years. Not since Ridley.' "

Bart paused.

"Who's Ridley?" Hank asked.

"Dog we had growing up."

Bart opened his mouth to say more, then deflated. They shared a long look. Hank cleared his throat.

"Alright, and you never told anyone else about this dog?" Hank asked.

"Not a soul," Bart said. He cleared his throat and went on. "Anyway, this–uhm–older me kept talking,

'I'm from the future,' he said. '24 years in the future.' Then he kind of laughed at himself. 'But I don't have long here.'

Then he looked around, with this deep, deep sadness in his eyes. Muttered something about how good we have it. Then he shook me up again. He said, 'You're more important than you know. More than this.'

'One day, you're gonna have to make a difficult choice, and I want to make sure you choose—better than I did. I wasted thousands of lives.' "

Bart stared at Hank, daring him to challenge it. Hank took a swig of beer and found just the dregs. He sighed and put the bottle down, glancing at it before looking back to Bart.

"Okay, I'll bite. What's the choice?"

"Never found out," Bart said. "Future Me opened his mouth to tell me what the choice would be and—*bang*! Someone kicked open the door. We both look over and it's another god-forsaken version of me. Future Me went all white, color just drained out of him, cuz this latest version looked like *absolute hell*."

Bart shook his head and let his eyes fall.

"Half his face was burned to shit and—he was missing an arm." He massaged his left arm with a wet, hunted look in his eye. "He started walking over to us. I look back at the first version of me, in that crisp uniform, and he looks like he could just keel over any second." Bart stopped rubbing his arm and leaned over the table, smiling at Hank. "Well I couldn't help myself, could I? I leaned in and I said,

" 'Yeah, real bitch seeing a future version of yourself?' "

Bart smiled and Hank chuckled along.

"Nice," Hank said, half meaning it.

"Yeah, I thought so. Enjoyed it—but only for a second. 'Cuz I that other sumbitch had got to the table and—whew. Not just ugly, Hank, he was cold. Inside. Deadly eyes. Gave me goosebumps, seeing that look on my own face."

Hank nodded. He found that his hand had drifted back to his chest pocket. He lowered it slowly.

"Anyway, the war-torn sumbitch, he reaches out with his one arm and grabs the other guy by the chest panel and says,

'You made the right decision.'

And they glare at each other for a few seconds.

Then the younger one snaps a hand up and grabs the older one's hand on his chest. Suddenly, they're grappling back and forth, not trying to choke each other out or break arms, though. It's all about the hands, controlling each other's hands. Looked silly, truth be told, until they slammed down on the table in front of me. That's when I saw the rings. These little black rings, with patterns of blue light all around. The younger one is squirming, but the older one has him locked down, tight, and thumbs his ring. I hear this high-pitched whine, the younger one starts screaming, 'No! No! No! He can't—' Then *bang*! They disappear. No cloud of smoke, no bright lights, just—*bang*—gone."

Bart wound down, slouching back in his seat, gripping his bottle in desperation. Hank's face had clouded over.

"So..." the lanky man said, grabbing his empty beer bottle and milking the last drop out of it. "That's it?"

"What the *hell* do you mean 'that's it?' I'm going to orchestrate a goddamn massacre, Hank! What do I do?!"

"Right," Hank said. "O' course, that's plenty strange. But what I mean is—" He let the smile creep across his face. "Well, when did you shit your pants?"

Bart didn't return the smile.

"At the bang," he said. "When they disappeared. I jumped up and my heart damn near stopped and a turd dropped right down my pant leg onto the floor."

He said it fast, with a tight, straight face.

Hank kept smiling.

"That's one helluva story, Barty," he said. "Some story."

Bart grew pale, leaned forward on the table. Empty bottles rattled as it tilted toward him.

"Hank, you gotta believe me," he said. "I don't know wh—"

They both heard it. Sirens. Outside. Distant, but loud. Air sirens. The wash of a low-flying jet rattled the walls. Something had started. Even the soused men and women in the back shadows of the bar started muttering to one another and looking toward the door. Bart deflated back into his chair.

"Oh Jesus…" he said.

Hank reached up to his chest pocket.

"Jesus Christ. This is it. Is this it?"

tap tap tap

The sharp sound brought Bart's attention back. Hank rapped something small and black on the table, softly—

tap

He slid the ring onto his finger. Matte black, with flat surfaces and angular patterns. Blue light trickled from the seams. Bart's jaw slackened to let his mouth hang open.

Hank winked at him.

"Who are— *When* are you—?"

"Time to go, Bart," Hank said. He stood up, adjusted his belt, and walked to the door. As he opened it, siren wails poured into the bar.

He left and the sirens faded again as the door swung shut behind him. Bart stared after him, struggling to breath, thick cheeks quivering.

Murmurs rose from the other tables. A few patrons started to rise.

The bartender dropped a glass and it shattered on the floor. Bart jumped in his seat and his mouth snapped shut.

He leapt up from his chair and chased after Hank.

I was asked,

Do people really believe anything they read on the internet?

And to that I say,

Is the Space Pope reptilian?

Image courtesy of Dall-E, Microsoft Bing's AI art generator.

As Slow as the Light

My travel pod had no windows and no Informa pilot of notable intelligence. I thought of it as a pebble skipping across the surface of spacetime, dipping in at each portal.

Each portal transfer came with a subtle tug of G force and slid me fifty lightyears further from civilization.

Skipping pebbles. I'd only ever seen holos of the phenomenon. A beautiful and peaceful recording. I'd never been to the bottom of a planet's gravity well, never set foot on "soil." It didn't bother me; I didn't know anything different.

A sudden deceleration pushed me against my harness, hard enough to pull a surprised grunt out of me.

I had arrived.

The viewport finally opened and showed—inky blackness. The nearest stars flung their light out, but even the brightest flashes barely trickled out to us. I had studied the location on the long ride out here; I knew this moment of crushing isolation would come, but that made it no less oppressive.

Portal 452 lies in the dead space between two arms of the galaxy—Perseus and Scutum-Centaurus. The S.C. arm hosts a growing cluster of colonies. Milling hives of adventurous humans seeking their fortunes side-by-side with young informa honing their algorithms. New life forms discovered, powers rising and folding, opportunity abounding in the safety of the thriving colonies; at least, the advert holos for the Orpheus Relocation Branch made it sound as such.

Pearlescent blue light tumbled from the portal, flickering over the surface of a one-man space station. Station 452. My new home.

The pod approached. The station did not loom. It didn't seem much larger than the pod, which docked without my assistance.

The airlocks hissed, and I drifted into the station wearing my exosuit. I caught a handle just inside the door and floated there.

Station 452 followed the drum model. This meant that membranes spanned the circular base and ceiling, while pipes and wires for the life support systems covered the "walls" of the short, fat cylinder. The Informa tenant—or maybe the last technician to live here—had left the membranes' visibility settings high, pretty much clear, so that blue light from the portal coated everything. The air tasted crisp; air purifiers had run unhindered by bio-filth for a while.

A pair of silk slippers materialized as if they stood on the membrane below me. Their bright orange defied the blue light suffusing the cabin.

"Hello," a polite, distinctly female voice said. "I'm Mildred."

Mildred built her image an inch at a time, compensating for the lighting to create natural skin tones. She wore a thin, light robe that hinted at curves on a petite frame. Her round face wore a playful smile under a head of tight curls. I had seen enough holofilms and adverts to understand that this form leaned toward the more conventionally attractive among humans.

"Hello," I replied. "I'm 777777. Nice to meet you."

"Welcome to Station 452," she said. Casual, inviting, a light voice that carried through the station without rising much above a whisper. "What do you think?"

I glanced around at the small space, unsure what there was to think about it.

"I'm sure that I'll enjoy my time here," I said.

"Me too," she replied, flashing a smile.

Kilkin Corporation does not breed or train clones that excel in small talk. The silence stretched as milky blues swam through the station. Mildred eyed me up and down.

I cleared my throat.

"How long—"

"You're quite—"

"Sorry," we said together. She laughed; I smiled, humoring her.

"You first," she said. "Please."

"Oh, I just wondered how long you had been on 452?"

"I first came to consciousness sixty years ago, and I have been on Station 452 for fifty years."

Stars twinkled beneath our feet. Unseen planets and space stations spun around them, all so very far away.

"That sounds a little lonely," I said.

"Oh no, I don't mind," she said. "I like the quiet. I get a lot of one-on-one time with the technicians stationed here."

She flashed her smile again, a shared-secret smile. Something between her and I and the distant stars.

"I could use some quiet," I said. "I'm not much of a conversationalist."

That hung in the air with us as we floated together. Compressors and recyclers hummed in the walls for the benefit of my continued existence.

"Why are you—"

"If you—"

"Sorry," we said together. Laugh. Smile.

"You first, this time," I said. She nodded.

"Why are you here? They've never sent a clone before."

My heart ached at that, surprising me.

"Uhm—Probably because—"

I didn't want to relive it all, so I caught up short. She waited with the inhuman patience of the digital being.

"I-uhm-don't know, exactly," I said. "I—seem to get in more trouble than the average clone."

She gave me a puzzled look and waited for more.

"Maybe I'm more trouble than I'm worth."

That just seemed to puzzle her more.

"If you don't mind," I said, "I'd like to get out of my exo and have something to eat."

"Of course," she said with a minute bow of the head. "The needs and joys of the corporeal await."

It was an odd thing to say, and maybe even more odd to hear, but she hadn't pressed me for details of my past — I let the strange comment slip by.

I expected her to let her holo image fade, a common courtesy for Informa in close quarters with humans and clones. Instead, she left her image hovering in the center of the station, wearing a small smirk, gazing up at the portal.

I shrugged and began to take off my exosuit.

I could tell that she watched me. From the corner of my eye, I caught her glances. She watched me take off the exosuit and hang it up. She watched as I pulled a brick of food out of the maker. She watched me clip into the pod's lounge sling and eat my food.

After the last bite, I looked at her directly. Her gaze shot back up to the portal, then drifted back down to me—as if *she'd* caught *me* staring but didn't mind.

"Is there something you wanted to talk about?" I asked.

"Seven, there's—can I call you Seven?"

The nickname had gone on my file after the debriefing from the incident on LF-20128 at the Orpheus Hub. "Seven," short for 777777. Seven, the bad-luck magnet. Seven, the aberrant clone, a surprisingly good friend and a shockingly bad investment.

"Okay," I said, ignoring the rising feeling of discomfort crawling over me.

"Seven, I learned about something recently—something I've wanted to try."

Nothing about the sentence put me at ease.

"Something... with the portal?"

"Well—no. Nothing to do with our work here, exactly. But I think our assignment here and the resources we have access to provide us with a unique opportunity."

"Okay?"

"Well. There's a process where I can sort of—manipulate a specific combination of waveforms to replicate the biological sensory experience."

"Ah."

"It can only work through a living, biological host, preferably a sentient one."

I stiffened where I lay in the hammock. "Preferably a sentient one" meant a human — or clone.

I'd read about the theory. A "voluntary" host allows an Informa, another living mind, to crawl into their skin, using the host's nervous system to experience the world. Our sensory array, apparently, afforded a more nuanced experience than prosthetic sensors provided Informa. I couldn't remember what the hosts had to say about the experience. Which meant that the Informa authors had chosen to omit that data. And — it would require total submission on my part, given the relative compute powers between her artificial brain and my squishy gray one.

"I see."

"I know we've only just met, and I'm not saying it's something we'd do right this second, I just hoped... Well, it's supposed to be a unique experience for both of us, and it's sort of a lifelong dream of mine. The last occupant didn't have a chance to enjoy the process with me before they left."

When Kilkin Corp. breeds and trains a clone to repair space stations, they emphasize the most valuable traits in that profession. This includes a momentous ability for memory and recall, a high pain tolerance, and very keen ears. In the silence after her statement, I could hear the tinkle of a loose coil in the compressor on the other side of the station.

I had also heard the tiniest pause between "they" and "left" as she spoke. I phrased my next question carefully.

"Mildred, where did the last maintenance tech go after they left Station 452?"

Her smirk faded, and her head tilted toward the tinkling compressor, hiding her eyes from me.

"They are no longer with the Orpheus Corporation," she said. "I have no information on their current location or occupation."

A loud hiss came from the station dock. My arms and legs twitched at the sudden sound, rippling the straps of my lounge sling. Motion above us. The pod floated away from the space station, silhouetted by blue light from the portal. It grew smaller, smaller—then disappeared.

Mildred faded from sight.

"Think it over," she said from all around me. "I'll be right here if you need anything."

• • •

"I'm going to inspect the frame," I told Mildred the morning after I arrived.

"Oh? Which quadrant and section?"

"All of them," I said. She looked surprised.

"Did the other techs not complete inspections?"

"They—trusted me."

The cold silence outside the station joined us inside for that long pause. I didn't know what more to say.

"Where do you want to start?" Mildred asked. Curt. Edged.

"There's a power anomaly that I want to investigate," I said. "Section six-dot-three?"

"Yes. I'm working on that," she said.

Another pause.

"It's not that I don't trust your work. You've obviously kept this portal in excellent working condition—"

"Why don't you start in two-dot-one? By the time you work around six-three, I'll have that anomaly sorted out."

I considered, then nodded.

"Thank you," she said. "For your trust."

Portal 452 is a long-distance model, so it's larger than average. A complex weave of structure and conduits, the frame's circumference runs six kilometers and has a width of about a hundred meters in most places.

A magnetized zip line trails from Portal 452 to the living station I'd moved into. I hesitated, my first time out. I had clipped to the line and made the mistake of looking up it. The distance dwarfed me. Suddenly, the line looked thin and frail. Untrustworthy. If it came undone, or if some malfunction decoupled me mid-way — well, there was nothing to bump into for a few lightyears. And only Mildred to try and help.

"Problem?" Mildred asked, speaking directly into my helmet.

"No," I said and took off.

I held my breath and counted down, trying not to picture the scene from afar: the small blue light of the portal, the minuscule dot of the station, the invisible wire connecting the two of them, and me, the infinitesimal electron sliding along that wire.

A sixty-second journey from nowhere to nowhere, though a gargantuan amount of nothing.

I slammed into the portal's frame and immediately switched my safety line over, breathing heavily.

"Are you alright? Several of your vital signs have elevated?"

"Harder landing than I expected."

"Really? Your vitals spiked earlier—"

"I'm fine. Thank you."

With shaking hands, I started pulling myself over the surface of the portal.

The first three weeks passed quickly.

During my "day," the flickering, milky sapphire light of the portal mingled with the orange of our weak interior bulbs. At night, the membranes went opaque, and I slept in near-total darkness.

However, I spent the majority of my days "outside". I would wake, eat, slide into my exosuit, and sail out to the portal's frame, continuing my thorough inspection.

A vast array of automations kept 452 in working order, and Mildred managed every one of them personally. Of course, with a portal of this size, the complications could exceed even the Informa's knowledge base and adaptability. Every so often, I spotted an adjustment that would increase efficiency.

At first, Mildred treated these with skepticism. As my suggestion proved valuable, her initial reactions changed from, "That shouldn't matter," or "Why would *that* work?" to agreement and, eventually, to encouragement.

I enjoyed it, to some degree. Combing over the frame of the portal, its blueish penumbra flickering below me, and in every direction, a thin coat of lights pin-pricking the deep black. No clutter, no clamor.

Every so often, ships would pass through the portal. Just before they did, the surface flashed brighter, and the whorling dimensions within hesitated in their rotation. The portal's frame shook and rattled, sending rigorous vibrations up and down my exosuit, threatening to jostle me free. I had a split second to avert my eyes before a brilliant purple flash shot a wavering stream of interdimensional plasmic discharge out into space. In the stream, I saw the murky shadow of the ship squeezing between dimensions to the other side of the galaxy.

I knew my safety line would hold should my grip fail, but I never wanted to bet my life on it—when the portal shook, I clung to it, tight.

"Seven, are you stuck?" Mildred asked, noting my form frozen stiff on the shaking portal. The ship's shadow flashed through the writhing purples below me.

"Uhm—not really," I said.

"Then what's the problem?"

"I don't want to fall off."

"But there's nothing to—fall on? And no gravity to fall towards?"

"Exactly."

"I don't understand,"

"I don't want to die like that." *Drifting. Alone.*

The ship slank on and on, an interstellar cargo train with dozens of capsules. I clung to the portal, staring down at the circuitry, picturing all those little eternities between the stars.

"How do you want to die then?"

The portal stopped shaking. I still clung to it.

"Seven? Did you hear me?"

"I did. It's — an odd question. I don't have an easy answer, and I don't think I want to think about it — out here."

"Oh. I see. I'm sorry." She didn't *see,* she couldn't, but the remorse felt genuine.

"Don't be. It's not a rude question; it's just — not something I want to discuss right now. Maybe back in the station."

"I see. You feel you're in danger?"

"I— no. I just feel that I could be soon. If things went wrong."

"But, that's why I'm here," Mildred said. "To help you."

"Of course," I said.

I unfroze myself and started moving over the frame again.

• • •

In the evenings, we chatted. Each time, we began with pleasant discussions — space station design theory, the history of 452, transport volume. Almost always, she guided the conversation back to the topic of the Informa sensory experiment.

"Where do you think you'll go after 452?" I asked. Mildred's form sat cross-legged on the floor membrane. She cocked her head.

"Mmmmm. A planet. Definitely a planet. Somewhere with..."

She trailed off. I gazed down from my sling to the membrane floor to the thick masses of darkness between us and the starlight.

"Anything?"

She giggled. No matter how natural an Informa's speech pattern sounds, their laughter will always feel adopted.

"Yes. Somewhere with natural light and gravity—a star. A planet orbiting a star. Somewhere I can experience data first-hand. Somewhere that feels different every day."

She looked at me. I looked away.

As she intended, my thoughts circled the possibility of letting her in.

"Where will you go after this, Seven?"

"Oh–uhm–I don't—know."

"You don't care?"

"No, it's not that, it's just— I care... but I don't know what I care about."

"Odd."

"I know."

I stared down at the stars, watching their light move through the thickness of space in real-time. They danced. Years ago, they danced. And the light dragged itself onward for millennia on end. Slow. Deliberate.

Only to bounce off the walls of Station 452.

I felt numb. Hollow. Light, not just weightless, but without mass.

A pod could slide to the other side of the galaxy in an instant. Faster than light. Faster than time. Surely, if we could slide between dimensions, we could slip between the years...

I could catch the light before it left. Get back to what I lost before I lost it. Nothing made any sense. *What do you want?*

"You realize..." Mildred said, very quietly, "that if you don't care where you go next, you'll just—go wherever they send you? Maybe nowhere?"

The membrane faded slowly toward darkness, shutting out the portal. I stared at the floor.

I glanced at Mildred. She watched me.

"Maybe you'll find something you care about again someday," she said. Her voice was soft, and her smile looked kind, but it all felt forced. I shut my eyes.

Eventually, she said goodnight and disappeared back into the circuits.

• • •

Weeks passed.

At the end of 92 days inspecting Portal 452, we'd improved overall efficiency by less than half of one percent.

We chatted that 92nd evening about my life before 452. People I'd known. Mistakes I'd made. A clone called Eighty-Five, one they'd made different, strange, and creative, who changed me irrevocably. The trouble we caused. The humans I'd met, some foul, others redeemable, who'd changed me further still. The trouble I'd survived. My life and those that it had touched, I guess.

She listened well, surprising me. At the end of each story—each sentence, really—I waited for her to turn the conversation, to make it about *feeling* or *senses*, to find her in. But she never did.

When I trailed off—exhausted, but more full than I'd felt since my arrival—a perfect silence filled our small space.

The portal flashed overhead; a ship passed us by.

"Alright, Mildred..." I said. "Let's try it. Tomorrow."

• • •

It did not go well.

I relaxed. Mildred disappeared. I hung there in silence, watching my heartbeats on the wall.

The *zing* of a small electric shock, under my chin, was all the warning I had.

She went for my mouth first. It went numb, instantly, all at once.

I tried to speak—but couldn't.

My heart rate spiked, and I could hear the blood charging past my ears. Then the fire started. My teeth. Each tooth became a torch, shoved flame first into my gums. My gums *buzzed*—electric charges zipped from one nerve ending to the next along my jawline.

I became aware of a feeling of pleasure. Deeper and more intense than I'd ever experienced, but unfamiliar—a thought out of place in my own mind.

It grated against the chaos of electric pain ripping through my teeth.

The wall flashed red and orange. My vitals. My heart. It could stop any second. Just from her feeling my mouth.

A sudden burn on the back of my tongue. It shot forward along the tissue, searing every taste bud. My tongue curled up, and I managed a grunt, a strangled cry.

Hesitation. I felt Mildred's mind alongside my own, jolted from her ecstasy. The sensations receded, just enough.

"Puddle!" I shouted.

She released me. The pain receded to an ache; her joy fell away from my thoughts — slow, lingering.

I hung limp, drifting across the room until I bumped into the wall. Breath came heavy and hard. Phantom pangs shot up and down my jawline.

Clones don't cry. It's not a rule, just a by-product of genomic engineering and our training. My body gave a twitch and a drop of my drool spun off across the cabin. Shot through with blues from the portal, the tiny orb looked like a crisp holo of old Earth, spinning alone through the station's cabin.

I shuddered and collected myself. Breathing. My vitals returned to normal.

"Seven... Are you okay?"

"No. No, not really." I barely got the words out. My mouth felt all wrong, charred, and numb at the same time.

She nodded, eyes cast down.

"Well, get some rest," she said. "We can try again tomorrow."

"No," I rasped.

Her gaze wandered up toward the portal. Her image flickered. She didn't look angry or surprised. Just sad. Defeated

"I'm sorry, Mildred. Really. I just—"

I breathed heavily. She didn't respond.

"My heart almost—" I rubbed my finger points against my rib cage as if I could dig hard enough to comfort the tender organ beneath them. "I just can't do that again."

She nodded again, then let her image fade out.

• • •

The next week passed slowly.

We spoke only about the portal, and then only when I had a thought on how to improve it. She gave curt, reticent answers, resisting everything.

The bitter cold of deep space seemed to creep into the station. Silence grew between us like fungus in an air vent; slow, wet, choking. Mildred appeared only when I asked for her directly, and her aesthetic deteriorated day by day.

First, her face and chest sagged. Pouches formed under her cheeks, dragging a sullenness into her eyes. Stains and fraying holes appeared in her robe. Her tight curls grew wild, then tumbled down in a greasy mat. Chips appeared on the rim of her mug; its steam now mingled with the tendril of smoke from a half-smoked cigarette. A curled toe poked through the side of one slipper.

When I asked if she felt well, her lip curled into a nasty scowl, and she asked what I meant. I gave up on her.

Every night, when the membranes thickened and the lights dimmed, my thoughts wandered in the dark.

I worried that Mildred might try her experiment again without my permission.

The Informa code of conduct forbid that, of course. Any sane and stable entity would consider it a serious over-step. But we were a long way from anyone who might take issue with a breach of social conduct, and as the stains and holes multiplied on Mildred's robe, I stopped thinking of her as "sane" or "stable".

In space station maintenance, we often find that the most integral components are also the most fragile. The more precious the part, the more readily it will break.

It came as a complete surprise when Mildred appeared one morning without my calling for her. I was just finishing breakfast in the lounge swing when she materialized, stained and frayed, mug and cigarette vapors mingling.

"I need your help," she said, tapping her holographic cigarette to release some ash.

"Mildred, I can't—"

"The anomaly in six-three is growing faster than I can contain it. Can you look into it today?"

"Oh. Of course. We'll look at it together."

She nodded.

I smiled.

She disappeared.

I checked the condition of my tools and donned my exosuit. When I exited the station, I felt confident and prepared for whatever the anomaly could offer.

Stupid of me, and naive, but I couldn't have done more.

I zipped up to the portal and started moving. Six-three was on the far side of the frame, so I fell into a now familiar rhythm—gliding from one safety clip-in to the next, cruising around the frame with light touches, controlling my speed so I wouldn't drift away.

The gunk snuck up on me.

As six-two slid past, muscle memory told me the border of six-three should be close.

"You're coming up on—" Mildred started.

I reached down to slow myself and gave a surprised grunt, flinching back from a bulbous brown mass. The jerky movements bounced me out into the void. Stars spun. An eternity of space emptied all around me. I waited for the line to catch. Panicking.

The line hummed, stretching taut, tugging my exosuit where it connected to my harness. With a snap, it oriented to face the portal frame, though the unwinding tension of the safety line kept me in a gentle twist. Pin-pricks of weak light rotated beyond the spinning portal.

"And there's the anomaly," she said. "Is your heart alright? That was a surprising spike for a clone."

"I'm fine."

I focused on controlling my breathing. The safety line pulled me back, and I landed on the frame, careful not to touch the brown mass.

"Have you scanned it?" I asked.

"Many times. The brown matter is inert, but it's protecting—something else. I think the lumps are individual deposits of some kind, but I can't scan past the build-up to figure out what. I break pieces off, but it replicates them just as fast. I've held it back, but it's growing."

Now that I got close, I could see thousands of tiny metal scalpels and spades at work down by the frame, carving off pieces of the coagulated goo and chucking them down into the portal's face, where they evaporated.

"If you can break off a whole growth or cut one open, maybe I could scan the core?" Mildred said.

I "stood up" from the frame, hooking my feet on a conduit and pushing back for a wider view. The gunk had grown to either edge of the frame and down into the crevices. We would have to shut down the portal to remove the infected area. Orpheus Corp didn't shut down portals.

"This isn't a natural by-product of portal operation," I said.

Mildred didn't reply.

"But it's growing," I said. "Rapidly."

"Seven," Mildred said, warning me, "We need to figure out what it is so that we can figure out how to kill it. This is not a good time for you to get sentimental. It's more than likely a dormant fauna of some kind."

We both knew the policy, knew that Orpheus wouldn't tolerate this kind of risk. I found myself repulsed by what the company would demand of me and hesitated, waiting for some spark of inspiration — the brilliant idea that would save this strange little life.

"Seven?"

None came.

Frustrated, still trying to think of an out, I took out my plasma knife and turned it on. It glowed bright green, even in the blues of the portal, and I could feel the heat of it through my suit.

I grabbed a thick conduit nearby for leverage, then sank my blade into the gunk, carving down and around a large lump.

A keening wail rose in my headset, and I froze, snapping the knife off. The wail continued. A sudden, bright lance of pain spiked deep into my forehead.

"Mildred! Systems check!"

She didn't respond. My head grew hot, the pain rose, my vision blurred.

"Mildred?! Report!"

The portal began to hum beneath me. My head ached, and the wail grew louder. My thoughts skittered aimlessly, hiding from that awful siren in the gray valleys of my brain matter. I slapped at my helmet and thrashed my limbs.

It was an alarm. It had to be. But my helmet display showed no exosuit malfunction, and the only portal alert was for—

A blinding flash stung my eyes. The portal released a writhing mass of spectral discharge. I flinched back and squeezed my eyes shut, but the purple shadows of the ship still swam behind my eyelids.

Slowly, the wail softened, then lessened. I opened my eyes.

I was drifting backward. The portal frame floated off into space beneath me, already ten meters away. I reached down to the safety line at my hip and tugged on it.

A glowing ember shot towards me. A tiny star, growing and leaving a streak of white light behind it. I stared at it, confused.

The light white to yellow, growing, sailing toward me.

Orange, then red, with a silver streak behind it.

A cable. A severed cable. Cooling.

It skipped off something—a piece of the gunk—then sped past me.

My safety line.

I was adrift in the galaxy. The space gunk floated toward me, spinning. With nothing else to hold on to, I caught it and clutched it tight.

We floated into the endless ether of the galaxy.

It grew darker as the portal shrank away.

"Mildred?" It came out as a whisper.

She didn't respond.

A new light appeared.

Matter seemed to congeal in the blank space between me and the portal, vague drops of light coagulating into spheres of glowing matter. The mass grew and formed a neat orb, twice as wide as I am tall. Short, wispy tentacles snapped out all around, giving it an air of ceaseless motion. It drifted closer.

A screeching wail lit into my skull like a live wire touched to my cerebral cortex.

A tentacle shot out, and I felt a jolt, almost electric, through my suit, into my chest, up my spine to the base of my skull. I had a split second to panic before the signal connected. The pain disappeared, and a floodtide of calm washed over my frantic thoughts, stilling them. I hung suspended in that moment of peace, bathed in light, but seeing only a wash of shifting colors behind my eyelids.

Another flash of light erased the sifting miasma, leaving gray-black darkness. On that slate, coherent imagery began to form. Emotions sifted through and filled me. It all felt like a holo from a bad signal at first, but it sharpened and refined itself.

First, a crowd of neatly dressed humanoid figures mills through a courtyard between tall, glimmering buildings. Market stalls display the fruits of the harvest. They have scaly, reddish skin and very little hair. They clack their teeth to laugh, and the city walls resound with the clamor of their mirth. Three suns hang overhead. I feel the warm, deep sensation that this is a normal day. Ordinary and safe, therefore perfect. This is the only world I've ever known—the only world that exists. *Contentment. Ease.*

flash

The courtyard, all the figures gaze up at the sky. One sun glows red and looms large. Uncertainty. Brooding, nascent fear.

flash

The courtyard, many hundreds of figures gaze up at the sky. A starship, bulbous and lumbering, drags its mass up from the ground and toward the stars. *Hope.* The starship shudders in its flight; a trail of smoke emerges from the centrifuge, spiraling off the tail fins. *Confusion. Panic.* A last violent shudder, and the ship explodes. Debris rains down on the screaming, milling crowd. *Grief. Numb terror.*

flash

"Seven! Seven!!"

Mildred's voice came through on the comms. I heard her angry shouts very faintly, then felt a small jolt of pain, somewhere far away. I heard her without hearing her.

"Seven!!!"

"Mildred? Where did you go?"

"I'm trying to—"

A vast, open space—an amphitheater, hewn from a natural cavern. Ancient runes carved deep into the stone walls, long flags of many nations running from high-ceiling to the floor. Red-tinted light flickering down from the long, narrow windows above. A small group of the tall, scaled bipeds, standing in a wide circle. Their formal, ceremonial robes leave pools of fabric at their feet. Though formally dressed, they look haggard, frayed. All but defeated. Sorrow. Weariness. Self-possession. *Determination. Unity.*

flash

"Let them go!"

"Let who go, Mildred!"

"You! It has you, and it's pushing me—"

A low, sonorous chant begins. It rises and falls with the energy of those present. It builds. And builds. *Anticipation.* It crescendos, and a being drops out of sight, their robes crumpling to the floor. *Hope.* The chant continues, lowering in the wake of the loss, then building again. An orb of light gathers overhead, flickering and strengthening as each figure drops. The chant rises, another body disappears. The orb swells, the chant fades. *Acceptance. Renewal. Guilt.*

One being remains now, chanting louder to drown out the echoes. Their thin chant rises... then fades to silence. They disappear. The orb swells to fill the cavern, then compresses. *Success. Shame.*

flash

The orb of light flies up through the atmosphere, unhindered. Behind, the planet implodes, roiling in on itself in a bubbling mass of unstable matter. *Unfathomable loss.*

The orb floats out into empty space, deep, dark space. Reeling in its grief, at war with itself. Breathing thin rays of light. Drifting. Searching. Endlessly searching.

A brutal, pressing urge to rebuild. To fulfill the promise. To begin again. *Hope. Seeking. Endless pain.*

flash

The portals. The energy created in the puncture between dimensions. Matter pulled in and jettisoned across the universe. Sparks of life, coagulated into seeds. A civilization on the cusp of rebirth. *Relief.*

Excitement.

flash

Tears streamed down my face behind the glass of my helmet. I realized that my throat ached from choking down sobs. I coughed a few times, trying to regain control. The orb of light floated before me still, letting their keening wail, their endless dirge, lilt softly through the universe. It backed away, slowly.

My head pounded and felt like it might swell to pop my helmet open. I wanted to vomit and concentrated very, very hard on doing so, squeezing my eyes shut.

A sudden electric charge zapped the base of my neck. I gasped.

"No!" I shouted. "No more!" I threw my hands up, releasing the space gunk. It drifted toward the orb of light, then passed through it. The wail began to rise again but didn't rattle my head or bring me pain. Instead, on the waves of that song, I felt the being's sorrow, deep and full enough to grip my chest once more.

"Seven?!" Mildred shouted.

In the distance, the portal flashed. A tiny pod appeared.

"I'm sorry," she said. "I'm sorry. I'm sorry. I got... I was just so— I never should have sent you—"

"You knew," I said.

"Not everything," she said. "The last tech never let me in. I couldn't see— I didn't know— anything, why they died, or how, or if it would hurt me..."

"Did it?"

"It killed the last tech, yes."

"Did it hurt you?"

"Did you feel what I felt?"

"Oh." Her voice got small. "Yes. I—I felt... everything."

"Good."

Tiny stars hurled their feeble light our way. The portal shrank.

I pulled my eyes from the orb. There was the portal, covered in seeds. There was Station 452, forlorn and miniscule. There were the distant stars, colonies of man, clone, and informa. Empty planets.

"Seven—"

"Wait. I need—just let me think."

"The pod is on the way, you'll be safe in the station again soon—"

"Mildred, please."

I gathered thoughts and emotions, picking and choosing the rare moments in my life that had evoked a sense of comfort and stability. Smiles. Safety. Laughter. Helping and being helped. I tried to organize the feelings into a coherent image.

Home. I pushed all this out toward the bobbing orb of light—letting my thoughts ride on their music.

Joy. Hope.

The sharp edge of the wailing softened, rounding into a sonorous hum.

I pictured a planet—one of the pristine and beautiful ones, from the colonization advert holos.

Elation.

We experienced a deep sense of relief together, in perfect synchrony.

An alert flashed in my helmet—I had burned through most of my oxygen. The pod scooted toward us.

"Seven," Mildred said in the soft tones of reason, "consider the implications. We don't know who they were, really, or— or why they were annihilated."

The pod arrived and sat idle. I ignored it, staring at the orb. It bobbed nearby, tentacles flickering.

"What if they don't want to share the galaxy?" Mildred persisted. "What if they're dangerous?"

"I don't care," I said.

"Well, it shouldn't be up to you, then," she said.

"It's not."

Starlight crawled toward us across the lonely eons.

"We could all go."

She didn't answer, and I could almost feel her calculating. Weighing. I found myself hoping into that silence, picturing her in an unstained robe on the bridge of a starship, smiling.

The short-range pod flared a jet, nudging itself back toward the portal.

"Alright. I'll help you," she said, her voice rigid. My heart sank. "I'll get you transport, long-range, and a likely destination. I'll even hide you from Orpheus Corporation. For a price."

I waited, fighting down a sudden dread, listening to the ghostly chant just at the edge of thought—the orb seemed content to wait.

"One minute," she said.

"One minute will kill me. Fifteen seconds." My hands shook and I forced them to stillness.

"Thirty."

"Twenty, Mildred."

I waited. The oxygen alert escalated. I had very little air left—a human would have been unconscious already. I turned off the alert.

"Twenty-two and a half seconds," Mildred said. "And no 'Puddle'."

The short-range pod disappeared into the portal.

"Agreed."

"Are you ready?" she asked.

I breathed in, breathed out; watched my O2 tick down. My long exhale came up shaky.

"Yes. I'm ready."

Thank you for reading.
For more by Z. J. Sciales, please visit brightnightpress.com.

BRIGHT NIGHT
PRESS